Cover by Gene Mollica

Editing by Lisa K.

To obtain permission to excerpt portions of the text, please contact the
author at www.becmcmaster.com

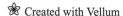 Created with Vellum

Kiss Of Steel

Heart Of Iron

My Lady Quicksilver

Forged By Desire

Of Silk And Steam

Novellas in same series:

Tarnished Knight

The Clockwork Menace

LONDON STEAMPUNK: THE BLUE BLOOD CONSPIRACY

Mission: Improper

The Mech Who Loved Me

You Only Love Twice

To Catch Λ Rogue

Dukes Are Forever

From London, With Love

London Steampunk: The Blue Blood Conspiracy Boxset 1-3

DARK ARTS SERIES

Shadowbound

Hexbound

Soulbound

Dark Arts Box set 1-3

BURNED LANDS SERIES

Nobody's Hero

The Last True Hero

The Hero Within

The Burned Lands Complete Trilogy Boxset

SHORT STORIES

The Many Lives Of Hadley Monroe

Burn Bright

SEDUCED BY DARKNESS

BEC MCMASTER

1

THIAGO

In the beginning there was Darkness.

It curls inside me, hungry and devouring. It takes little nibbles of my soul, day by day, even as I fight against it. I've chained it deep within me, binding it with magic and wards, tattooing them into my very skin to keep it locked away, but I can feel it straining against the edges of those wards.

It's all I've ever known.

I stare into the mirror in my tent, trying to see if there's a little bit more of it showing in my eyes. They're black right now as I strip the glamor from my skin, revealing the creature inside. Black wings spread wide, glossy with feathers. Dark claws are sharpened to points on my finger-tips. My eyes are black. Pure black. And even though the shadow daemons I've consumed writhe across my skin, my wards flare gold like a net draped over me.

Safely locked away.

But that doesn't mean I can't feel them gnawing at me.

1

It doesn't mean I can't feel my own roaring hunger threatening to consume me.

The Darkness feeds on anything. Anger. Pain. Torment. Fury.

And right now, I am all of those things.

"No, you're not," I whisper to my reflection as I dry my hands and wrists with the towel and toss it on the vanity. "You're more than a monster."

I am Thiago of Evernight, ruling prince of a kingdom that hates me, spawn of a creature so vile I can't even name it, and a bastard usurper who hides behind his illusions.

Keeping the Darkness contained within me is a daily battle, and I'd like to say the pressure of the current situation—a friend currently held hostage by my enemy—is the reason I can't quite look myself in the eyes right now, but there's another truth beckoning.

My father is thinking of me.

I can feel him somewhere far to the north of me, in Unseelie, where the wild fae live.

For the first time the hunger relents. It wants to be whole. It wants to consume him.

But destroying my father means confronting him, and for the first time the creature within me knows fear.

"Thiago?"

Not alone.

I vanish the wings, the claws, the blackness in my eyes. It's as simple as taking a step sideways, into the ever-present glamor I first conjured when I was a boy. Sometimes it feels like this is the real me, the one who smiles at the world with his handsome face. The one who can meld into any Seelie court without having his parentage questioned. The eyes that meet mine in the mirror are green now.

The handsome prince is back, the monster contained.

A pity I can feel him still, laughing under his breath as I turn to face the intruder.

Him, he whispers mockingly in my head. *Are we still trying to pretend I'm not you?*

The only way to deal with it is to ignore it.

"Eris?"

There are few people who are allowed into my inner sanctum like this, and Eris of Silvernaught is one of them. Tall, broad of shoulder and hip, her dark skin lit with the gilded light of the candle, she knows a thing or two about the monster within.

There's a look in her eyes that tells me she saw my eyes. "Thiago—"

"I'm fine." There's no point dwelling on it. I've spent years controlling myself. I will chain it down deep inside me again. I reach for a shirt and haul it over my head. "Are the others ready for me?"

"As ready as they're going to be." She growls under her breath as she reaches out to yank my shirt into place. "You're losing weight. You need to eat more." A sharp nail digs into my ribs in order to make her point. "And you need to tell me when your wards are on the verge of breaking."

"I will. I'm not that close."

"Close enough," she replies. "I need to *know*, Thiago."

Because she's my failsafe.

If my wards break and the daemon inside me is

3

unleashed, then Eris is the one who will kill me. I made her promise such a thing years ago, when I first rescued her from an unforgiving alliance of queens.

A shudder runs through me. That promise is the only thing that gives me any peace at night, but sometimes I'm not even sure if she *can* kill me.

It's so fucking hungry right now.

I force myself to imagine a set of dark eyes, framed by thick lashes. Maybe brown. Maybe blue—as dark as the color of midnight. The rest of the face is slower to form—it's been over five centuries since Maia granted me an image of this face, and while I've been carrying it for this long, hoarding it within my heart like a dragon guarding its treasure, the edges are starting to blur.

She's beautiful.

Large, serious eyes that absolutely light up the second she sees me and smiles. It's the smile that does the damage. It reaches down deep and clenches its fist around my heart. Her face is heart-shaped with a faint cleft in the middle of her chin, and hair like dark silk cascades over her bare shoulders.

The goddess Maia doesn't often grant favors for those who pray to her, but this one night when I was at my lowest, kneeling in her temples with my knees wet with my blood, she gave me a shred of hope.

She showed me the face of the woman I'll marry.

The woman I will love.

It's enough to force the jagged remnants of my father's shadow from my heart.

He can't defeat me here, with the image of my future wife reaching out a hand toward me as if to lead me into some future adventure. Not even the Darkness can overwhelm me right now.

She's my hope. My shield. The only fucking thing that keeps my chains of control in place.

"I'm fine," I repeat again.

"You're such a stubborn bastard." Eris tosses my cloak at me. "The others are waiting. Thalia's little birds have come in."

"There's news of Finn?"

"There's news." She stalks toward the flap of canvas that partitions this room off from the main tent. "Whether it's good or not is a question only Thalia can answer."

It has to be good. I won't accept any other outcome.

PUSHING THROUGH THE CANVAS FLAPS, I FIND THE MAIN room of the tent filled with my people.

They're all here.

My generals, my spymistress, my friends.

There's just one empty chair and it belongs to Finn.

The twins, Baylor and Lysander, look like matching monoliths carved out of stone, but despite that it's easy to tell them apart.

Half of Baylor's silvery-blond hair is drawn into a leather thong, the rest hangs down his back in messy tangles. His armor is scarred green leather, braids of it overlapping the enormous breadth of his chest. But it's the scowl that identifies him. Baylor's never met a smile he wouldn't drag into a back alley and stab to death.

Lysander, on the other hand, is all wickedness and

5

flashy grace. Clad in a black velvet doublet that sets off his hair, his cheeks are smooth-shaven as well as one side of his head. The rest of his hair hangs in a silken fall over the right side of his face. It makes his cheekbones look sharper and sensual, and rings glitter on his fingers. It's a little fancier than his usual attire, but Lysander likes to party and the queensmoot—a centuries-old meeting between the heads of the Seelie Alliance—is renowned for three days of drinking, dancing and fucking.

Secret assignations between members of opposing royal courts are common. It doesn't matter who you serve when the bonfires that bring in Lammastide are lit.

It's the only time of the year when ancient enmities are set aside and the fae can give in to our hedonistic natures.

There's no sign of pleasure on any of their faces. This Lammastide is different.

Because, while old arguments must be set aside for the duration of the queensmoot, it doesn't mean that blackmail and murder don't occur—just as long as they can't be tied back to your camp.

And right now, the Queen of Asturia has a knife to my throat.

It's Thalia I turn to, pressing a kiss into her hair. "You have news?"

We share a grandmother and while there's a hint of me in her sable brown hair and devious eyes, her managing ways are all her own. This is where the threat comes from, despite the pretty purple velvet gown and the innocent curls that tumble down her back. Nobody would ever suspect she's my spymistress and while she can't kick a man's head off his shoulders the way the others can, she's a knife in your back when you least expect it.

She tilts her head back. "I have news."

Thalia's never this serious, so whatever it is, it's trouble.

"Tell me," I murmur, circling the table.

"Adaia has arrived in all her golden glory," Lysander replies. "I managed to get a good look at the layout of the Asturian tents. She's set up in her usual spot and while there are numerous tents for her guards and servants, there's nothing that looks like it's built to hide Finn."

"He's there," Thalia counters. "Rue caught a glimpse of him."

She's spent years cultivating the tiny winged demi-fey that flutter through the castle at Ceres, which is home. They're addicted to milk and honey, and will do practically anything in exchange for it, but to get them to focus on one task long enough to complete it is near impossible.

My cousin has a stubborn streak though. And immortality has its uses. According to her, she's trained an entire legion of the little winged sprites, and considering the depths of the information she always manages to uncover it's hard to doubt her.

"Rue has the brains of a thimbleful of mead," Lysander replies. "I can't see any sign of Finn, and I'm *good*. I can't smell him. And I've heard no mention of him among the Asturian troops."

Thalia sniffs. "It's not my fault you're incompetent."

"*Incompetent?*"

This needs to be broken up before they're shouting at each other. I shift, but Baylor beats me to it, one enormous

7

fist slamming into his brother's chest and pinning him there.

"Finn," Baylor says pointedly, "is all that matters."

Lysander curses under his breath, shooting Thalia a dirty look from beneath his thick lashes. "I'm going to have an apology from you later, brat."

"I didn't see the army you rode in at the head of."

"Thalia." I settle a stare upon her that makes her sigh and draw her knees up to her chest. Her feet are bare, but the girlish look she shoots me slides off me like water.

I know her too well to fall for this innocent bullshit.

I also know the strain that exists within the room is real.

We're all on edge.

Finn's usually the one to break the tension, and Lysander—always by his side—is feeling it.

There are always risks in the game of kings, but I hate this moment, when the risk doesn't pay off. Asturian soldiers were seen sniffing around the ruins of Mistmere. The kingdom was destroyed during the war with the Unseelie five hundred years ago, and it's been a point of contention between me and Adaia for centuries.

I don't even want the fucking kingdom, but I can't let that bitch get her hands on it. With Mistmere under her domain, Adaia will own the entire western flank of Evernight, cutting us off from the rest of the Seelie alliance. Trapped in the north by the indomitable mountains that lead to Unseelie, the only access we'd have to the south is by the seas.

And it wouldn't surprise me if Adaia has conjured a

means to see any ships we send south don't arrive at their destination.

I can't let her have Mistmere.

And there's no reason her guards should even be seen in its forests. She's up to something and I need to know what it is.

Finn was supposed to track them and keep watch.

Except he vanished and Adaia sent me a message promising she'll exchange his head for the keys to the kingdom. Whether it's still attached to the rest of him is up to me, apparently.

We'll discuss it at the queensmoot, her message had practically purred.

"She has Finn with her." It's not a question. "She wants to use him to break me, and she'll want him close enough that she can get to him if she needs to."

"Maybe she's keeping him in her tent," Baylor growls.

Lysander shudders. "Brother, please. My *imagination*."

Baylor arches a brow at him. "Adaia won't fuck him. She considers his kind to be beneath her."

"Yes, but that doesn't mean she won't be fucking someone else—and I did catch a glimpse of the queen's pet on my prowl." Lysander's lip curls. "I don't know what would be worse. Watching the Queen of Asturia in bed, or being in it."

"Definitely being in it." Eris looks disgusted.

"What did Rue say about him?" I ask Thalia.

"The demi-fey don't talk, so it's kind of like…. Big, growly warrior. Cage. Something about a wolf prowling around in there. Poison. Stink—"

"*Poison?*"

9

Thalia smooths her skirts. "Iron, I suspect. They consider it to be poison."

A fair assumption, considering what iron can do to fae magic. It's difficult enough to touch it myself. The sudden grip of nausea makes even the strongest glamor slip and fade. It's like trying to hold moonlight in your cupped hands.

Finn's in a cage. An iron cage. Nauseous and sick with it. Shaking violently. Trapped in the iron sickness that makes your head throb and your thoughts dangerous.

Sudden rage makes the daemon slip its leash.

We could kill Adaia, it whispers. *The iron won't stop* me. *Nor will her magic.*

Or anything else for that matter.

I shudder the thought away. This is how it tempts me. It sounds so reasonable. But I've been there when I blink my way back into control of my body and find the blood covering my hands. I've seen the bodies, heard the sobs. I've tasted the sick slick of that desire on my tongue.

Let's burn it all to ashes. Let's kill them all.

Control is the chain I bind myself with.

It's what I used to lock my heart away when I held my dying mother in my arms, her blood slicking my shirt to my chest. It's the whip I flogged myself with during the bloody war against my half-brothers, when they sought to name me her murderer and pledged to turn my kingdom against me.

It's imprinted on my soul, tattooed into my skin. A cage I worship when the daemon threatens to chew me up and spit me out.

And it's what I fall back on now as I separate my

thoughts from the hot flush of emotion. I can't afford to give in to anger. Not right now. Finn needs me at my best. Not distracted. I owe him nothing less.

"We can't get to him through violence." Cutting our way through the Asturian delegation will only bring the fury of the entire Seelie alliance down upon my head. The queensmoot is sacred. The ruins of Hammerdale are neutral ground. To go against that ancient pledge means spitting on everything I've spent years cultivating. "And Adaia won't give him back to me, unless I beg. She wants me on my knees. She wants Mistmere. And I don't dare give it to her."

"There is… some leverage we might be able to wield against her. Adaia has both her daughters with her this year," Thalia murmurs.

I met the eldest daughter last year. Andraste is the spitting image of her mother, and from the haughty arrogance she greeted me with, I daresay she's inherited her mother's mean streak and air of privilege.

"What's the name of the youngest?"

"Iskvien," Thalia replies. "I don't know a lot about her. My resources say she's not as favored as the eldest. Adaia hasn't announced an heir yet, but Andraste is the frontrunner. There's rumor that the youngest daughter's magic is weak."

Adaia will hate that.

Strength is power in this world, and she's spent centuries building a stronghold out of her alliances and magic. To have birthed a daughter with barely any magic will be an embarrassment for her. No wonder I've never seen this Iskvien before.

She's probably another little clone of her mother. Blonde. Cruel.

Unimportant.

Or... is she?

I prowl around the table, unable to sit. "Right now, Adaia has a hostage. We could even the playing field."

Lysander leans forward, the front legs of his chair hitting the ground. "You want to kidnap a princess of Asturia?"

"Without bloodshed?" Even Eris's eyebrows arch. "*Here*?"

"Mmm." It's dangerous. Reckless. It could cost me everything. But it could also neutralize Adaia before she can make a single demand of me. "I want eyes on her daughters. Don't be seen. Don't harm them. I just want to know where they are and who they talk to."

"They could be innocent," Thalia retorts.

"Adaia's daughter?" Maybe I believed in innocence once upon a time, but years of strife and bloodshed have burned such notions from my heart. There's no innocence left in this world.

And certainly not within the heart of the Asturian court.

"I'll take the eldest," Lysander says.

Baylor scowls. "Fine. I'll track down the youngest daughter."

"It's one thing for Adaia to take Finn hostage in the ruins of Mistmere," Thalia points out as if we've all lost our minds. "Quite another to *kidnap* a royal princess right in the heart of the queensmoot."

"I think it's perfect," Lysander replies. "Everyone will

be wearing masks. They'll all be mingling and drinking. Nobody is even going to know if we take her."

Thalia leans forward. "She arrived with Adaia. Even Prince Kyrian is going to arch a brow in surprise if she suddenly appears in our encampment, and he's our ally."

"Then someone 'seduces' her," Lysander suggests. "Maybe she's enjoying our hospitality? The only one who needs to know the truth is Adaia."

"Are you volunteering?" Thalia asks.

"As handsome as I am," he retorts, "everyone knows my preferences lie elsewhere. Someone... else...." He scans the room, his gaze drifting between me and Baylor.

Baylor gruffly folds his arms over his chest and glares at his brother. "Have you been drinking already?"

"That's a no. Nobody would believe it." Lysander steadies his focus upon me.

"I don't *do* seduction." Somehow the words come out a little roughly. "Particularly not with the enemy's daughter." I snap my fingers at Thalia. "Eyes on her only. For now. But she might be a bargaining chip we can use. What else do we have?"

"Well, there's the matter of the Ravenal alliance."

The words near take my feet out from under me. This was a private matter discussed between the two of us—and I certainly never gave her permission to reveal it to the others.

"Ravenal alliance?" Eris asks.

"The queen of Ravenal has a granddaughter," Thalia explains to the others. "Her name is Lucere and—"

"And this was supposed to be a consideration only," I snap. "What in the name of Maia have you done?"

"Princess Lucere is of marriageable age," Thalia continues to the others, as if I haven't spoken. "She is also interested in meeting our prince at the queensmoot." She gives me a stern look. "You said you would consider the alliance. Lucere only wants to meet you to see if you would suit."

"Marriage is the last thing on my mind right now," I growl out. "Finn must be our first priority—"

"Finn *is* our first priority," Thalia snaps. "But if he's the only hand of cards we're playing right now, then Adaia will have us backed into a corner quicker than you can say, 'Yes, Adaia. No, Adaia. How high would you like me to jump, Adaia?' Let's open negotiations with Adaia and see what she wants in exchange for him, which means we must relay this through the Seelie Alliance. Everything we do to get him back must be played out in the open, or she'll kill him and have perfect justification to do so."

Her voice softens. "Prince Kyrian is our only ally. The other queens think you're an upstart prince who stole his throne. You *need* allies. More allies. You need someone to back you when Adaia comes for your throat. You need someone who might vote your way if Adaia pushes the issue. With Queen Maren of Aska in bed with Adaia, that only leaves Lucidia of Ravenal. The old bitch is cunning. She knows she's no powerhouse, but she also knows we need her. With Evernight to the north of Asturia and Ravenal to the south, Adaia will barely dare to breathe. It's our only hope. Meet with Lucere. Marriage to her could be the means with which we get Finn back without bloodshed."

"I know, but…."

She's out there. The woman I'm meant to marry.

Maia wouldn't have granted me a glimpse of her face all those years ago, if she meant me to be bound to another.

Something softens in Thalia's eyes. She alone knows the truth of what I saw. "It's been five hundred years since you were granted that vision, Thi. If she was out there—"

"If she's out there," I grind out, "then I can't bind myself to another. I *can't*." Not even for my country.

Not even for *Finn*?

My breath catches. I know the answer to that. He's my brother-at-arms. My ally. My friend. Five hundred years ago he saved my life on the battlefield and I can never repay that.

"I will… meet with Lucere." Even saying those words feels like dying a little on the inside.

For five hundred years I've been holding onto a dream, clinging to it at times with the desperate need of a man hanging from the edge of a cliff by his fingertips.

I can't give up.

The woman I saw has to be out there somewhere.

But if this is the cost of Finn's freedom….

He saved my life.

Can I do any less?

2

ISKVIEN

The first day of the queensmoot dawns bright and golden as my mother's servants set up the tents. Asturian colors flutter in the breeze as a warning as to whose quadrant this is.

Beyond them rise a sea of tents, clinging to a gently sloping hillside that envelops a circular valley. The tents of the Seelie Alliance stretch almost halfway around the valley. The sight makes my breath catch.

There are hundreds of fae here.

Thousands.

And tonight they will sing and dance and seek to drive away the restless spirits that haunt Arcaedia on nights like these. I've seen paintings of the queensmoot and heard all the tales, but this is the first time I've ever attended.

Asturia is granted the land right on the flank, and everywhere you look there's a sea of red and gold. My mother's rose, thorn and crown standard rises above her tent. She's somewhere within, no doubt plotting ruin for some poor soul.

I don't want to know.

I never want to know what she's up to.

That doesn't mean I always get my wish.

Beside us stands the Askan encampment with its golden serpent leering from a dark green background.

And then the burgundy of Ravenal, with a black crow picked out in stark relief upon their flag.

The blue and silver of Stormlight is next, and right at the end, as far away from the Asturian camp as one can possibly get, squats the sinister black and silver of Evernight.

I can see the moon in eclipse on their banners. It looks like some malevolent wolf swallowing down the sun. Seven stars twinkle in the black velvet; one for every tear that Roswyn, a long-dead queen of Evernight, shed when a curse settled over her kingdom, drawing endless night down over the north of her country.

A shiver runs through me as I tear my gaze away.

Best not to look to Evernight, even though I can't help being insatiably curious.

Their murderous prince is wicked, cruel and unrelentingly handsome, according to my sources.

He's also my enemy, inherited from my mother.

I desperately want to explore the ruins that run rife through the surrounding forests, but the risk is too great with Evernight here. Mother told me not to go too far, but everyone is busy setting the tents, and I was shooed out of the way when I tried to assist.

A footstep behind me is the first warning I'm not as alone as I think I am.

Hands clap over my eyes, and a hard body steps into

mine from behind. "Surprise, Princess."

Panic beat its wings in my chest the second I feel those hands, but at the sound of his familiar voice every inch of me goes still.

Etan.

It's been two years since I saw him last. And yet I'd know that voice no matter where I am. My body can't help reacting—all those practiced touches he bestowed upon me tamed it like a beast to the halter—but it's my heart that drives a wretched mallet through the shock, and forces me into action.

"*I love you, Vi.*"

Yeah, almost as much as you love power.

"*I want you to be mine. Forever.*"

Pretty little lies. Blessed Maia, I don't know how I believed it for even a second.

He'd been too good to be true. He was still too good to be true.

And if I hadn't overheard him that day, fucking a sprite I'd later discovered was his mistress and laughing about the foolish little princess he had wrapped around his finger, then I'd probably still be following him around Queen Maren's court like some lovesick fool.

"Etan." I duck out of his clutches, spinning around. "What are you doing here?"

Each queen in the Seelie alliance—or prince, for there are two of them—is granted a certain coterie to attend them. Fifty guards. A hundred of their inner court. Thirty servants. Ten family members at most.

No more. No less.

There are appearances to be kept and wars to be

avoided, and it results in five very carefully kept apart camps spread around the ruins of Hammerdale.

Etan might be the Queen of Aska's distant nephew, but he's hardly one of her favorite relatives—nor is he crucial to the alliance talks. He's a professional courtier it seems, currying favor wherever he can find it, and Queen Maren knows it.

I thought I'd be safe.

"Looking for you," says the tall, handsome fae lord grinning at me.

Etan of the Goldenhills. It's a name I once scrawled in the margins of countless notebooks. I hate myself for that. I knew better. I was raised as an Asturian princess. I should have seen through him.

But I was sixteen, lonely and sentenced to a foreign court where I knew nothing and no one, and his was the first kind smile I'd seen.

I spent a year serving Queen Maren as her lady-in-waiting; a little negotiation between my mother and the sister-queen she kindly calls the Queen of Nightmares. Long ago, Maren was named my godmother, and though she's never been the kind to bestow kisses and advice, there was always a birthing day gift. Always a present at winter solstice. To have her as a godmother was an honor.

It was never a kindness.

But the second I saw Etan he took my breath away, and my thoughts along with it. He swept me into a world where I was finally welcomed by the young swains who ruled Maren's under court. There were balls. Music. Dancing. Stolen kisses in the hedge maze that guards the gardens.

Even after two years apart, he still takes my breath, if I'm to be honest with myself.

Tall, lean, built like a powerful warrior fae, his skin kissed by the sun and his hair as golden as wheat beneath a blistering sun, he looks every inch the fairy tale prince.

Truth be told, once I realized he was playing me, I found the charms and potions on his vanity that help veil him.

Belladonna to darken his eyes, crushed pearl to brighten the inside of his lids, and powdered gold swept through his hair—it all plays its part and it's common to see the likes of such powders among the Seelie courts. But it was the little vials with trapped Will-o'-the-wisps that made my breath catch.

The tiny demi-fey are spirits of light. Some of the poorer villages in Seelie use them for lighting—trapping them within lanterns, or bartering with them to exchange milk and honey for several hours of their assistance.

But it's said that in Unseelie, the creatures there have discovered a darker use for them.

Their magics are small but if you can consume that magic, then the effect of it will brighten your skin and hair for a week. It's a tiny surge to your powers, but they say it's addictive and such magic has long been outlawed in Seelie.

I can see it in Etan now.

The natural warmth of his smile, the glow of his skin— it's all a lie—and it's used as bait in order to lure someone like me into his trap.

Hunger shadows his eyes as he stalks toward me. I don't know how I didn't see it before—or maybe I didn't want to. I wanted to believe the sweet lies he whispered in my ears. I wanted to let every gentle kiss he bestowed upon me steal me away from the wretchedness of my life. I wanted the white knight, the handsome prince, and when Etan appeared, blinding in his gloriousness, I let myself overlook the shadows etching his soul. He was a dream I refused to examine too deeply, and maybe I own some share of the blame in what became of us.

Because I wanted that lie so desperately that I let myself overlook the warning signs.

"You left my aunt's court so precipitously," Etan says. "You didn't even say goodbye."

"I'm surprised you noticed." I can't stop the hint of acid from flavoring the words. "You seemed to be cock-deep in a sprite the last I saw of you."

"Ah. You saw that." He doesn't look entirely surprised. "Can you blame me? You'd been playing games with me for months. A male has certain needs, Iskvien, and you were playing coy."

"I was doing nothing of the sort!"

He scoffs. "What else am I to call it? You would barely kiss me, let alone slip into my bed—"

And to think I was going to gift this bastard my virginity. "I wasn't sure if I could trust you—instincts that have served me well, in hindsight. I thought you were…."

"What?" Another step closer.

"Wooing me," I snap. "I thought you were falling in love with me."

Etan laughs. "Oh, Iskvien. What is love compared to the game?" His gaze sharpens, becomes a little cruel. "Your innocence was amusing then, but there's only so

21

long before a man grows bored." He runs his tongue over his teeth. "I think I like this better. Now you know. Now you're no longer looking at me as if I ought to cast my handkerchief at your feet and beg your favor."

"No, I'm looking at you as if you're an utter pig who isn't fit to kiss the hem of my skirts."

"Careful now, Princess." Maybe it's not Belladonna widening his pupils. Maybe it's something worse, because the merest hint of my defiance unleashes a feral kind of hunger in his expression. "This spitfire attitude makes the chase interesting again but you *will* respect me."

I don't know what it is about him that makes me uncomfortable in that moment, but I take a half step back when he advances upon me.

I know how to use the dagger sheathed at my hip, and I'm safely within Asturia's camp, but the makeshift streets are suspiciously empty for this time of day. Canvas flaps in the breeze, but I can't even sight so much as a hob.

I'm alone.

"I hate you," I say firmly. "I'm not interested in being chased. I don't ever want to see you again. Remove yourself from these tents. You're trespassing."

He reaches out and tries to brush his finger down my cheek, an ugly smile dawning when I jerk back. "Then it is truly a shame that my aunt and your mother have reached an agreement."

For a second, I'm not sure if I've heard him correctly. "What?"

"There's to be a marriage to cement the alliance between our countries." He captures my chin, pinching a little. "You're mine, you frigid little bitch. I will have you on your knees. I will have you on your back. I will have you locked in a fucking cell if I so choose. Maybe I'll even fuck you in front of my court—"

"Never!"

I strike his hand away, but the ache of his touch lingers in my skin.

"Go," he mocks. "Run to your mother. Ask her if it's true. My queen is signing the contracts today and once they're signed you belong to me, Iskvien. Now and forever." His gaze runs down my body. "Maybe you should wait for me tonight. I'll find your tent and you can beg for my forgiveness."

Heart pounding in my ears, I whip my dagger free and point it at him. "If you even take a single step within my tent, I'll cut your heart out of your chest and give it to your queen in a box."

His eyes light up and he laughs. "I'm glad we've had this little chat. This is much more interesting than having you simper at me like some little lovesick swain."

I can't breathe.

My mother wouldn't do this to me.

She *wouldn't*.

But I can't help thinking of her close ties with Maren of Aska. Mother's been murmuring about an alliance with the Queen of Nightmares for months.

War is on the horizon. She's already sent her troops marching north to hold the borders against the encroach of Evernight. Their murderous prince has been making aggressions, and the lands of Mistmere have long been in dispute between them.

I stare at Etan as he blows me a kiss and backs away.

23

"Until tonight," he says. "Save me a dance at the rites. No. Save them *all* for me. Once we are married you will never touch another fae again."

Mother won't care if I go bursting in there demanding the truth. I'm her daughter, and she's been hinting that my virginity is worthless to the kingdom if I never plan to gift it.

This is exactly something she would do to me.

I know it as surely as I know that marrying Etan will be a worse nightmare than my current life at court.

My mother has sold me.

To a monster.

"Over my dead body," I whisper, but there's no one here to hear it.

"ARE YOU COMING?" ANDRASTE CALLS AS SHE SLIPS within my tent. "Mother's gone to the queensmoot's opening ceremony. We're supposed to—"

My sister's voice cuts off as she notices I'm not even dressed, my hair hanging in tangled knots over my shoulders. I've spent the last two hours pacing, trying to think my way around this.

"Vi." Andraste's brows furrow. She looks like a miniature version of my mother. Tall, blonde, blue-eyed. "What are you doing? The first bonfires are being lit at any moment. Mother wants us to be there for it."

Traditionally, the three Seelie queens light the bonfires that bring in Lammastide. It hearkens back to a time when the fae went to war against the Old Ones and the otherkin who ruled Arcaedia before the fae arrived; night was a time of mischief and murder, and fire was used to ward them off.

The first time the fae lit the bonfires and sang in the equinox the way they did in the home world, there was a bloody ambush.

The otherkin fight with fangs and claws, and knives chipped from obsidian or stone. They hunt in packs and prefer ambush over outright confrontation.

And the first time Lammastide darkened the skies, when the fae were merry and drunk, the otherkin slipped from the forests and attacked.

Hundreds died until Blessed Maia and the other fae queens joined their powers together and fueled the fires with their magic, until the otherkin were blinded by the sudden light and left defenseless. The fae retaliated and drove them back, but now we always remember to light the bonfires.

It is an honor for my mother.

It's a moment where she and her sister queens will stand in power before all the fae assembled.

And it forces her hated enemy, the Prince of Evernight, to bear silent witness as she reigns supreme.

I don't give a damn about any of it.

"Did you know?" I stare at myself in the mirror, clad in my underthings.

There's a pair of dresses laid out on the bed behind me.

One is green and gold—the colors of the Goldenhills, now that I know the game is afoot. Mother gifted it to me weeks ago. It's another slap in the face to know this has been going on for at least a month, and I was completely unaware of it.

"Know what?" my sister asks.

"That she's sold me to Etan," I snap.

Andraste pauses, her gaze sliding over everything. It returns, hesitantly, to me. "I thought you were enamored of him. You wrote of him when you served in Queen Maren's court. You seemed… to bear feelings for him."

I can't stop myself from pacing. "That was before I came to *know* him. He found me today in the tents. He…." I bite the words off. "Marrying him would be… unpleasant."

Andraste's eyes sharpen. "Did he threaten you?"

"He practically said I would be his property."

"Mother's signed the contract," she says slowly. "All it requires now is your signature. It was supposed to be announced on the final night." Her mouth tightens. "I thought you knew."

How? I can't stop my gaze from lifting to meet hers in the reflection.

Mother barely speaks to me, and Andraste is too fucking busy with her little court within courts to have time for me.

The courtiers all know which way the wind is blowing.

I'm the queen's unfavored daughter.

Without magic. Without power. Not even half as pretty as my mother and sister.

And Andraste is angling for the position of heir. She's built a small court of courtiers around her—the Crown Princess's Larks, they call themselves. An unofficial title, but one which I'm certain is not too far away.

I don't know where that leaves me.

"Here." Andraste pushes me into a seat and gathers my hair into a pile on my head, twisting sections of it into place and considering it. Those blue eyes wear the weight of a thousand years, and sometimes I wonder what she's seen at court. "Let me fix your hair. Mother will have your head if you appear looking like this."

It's been years since we've even touched.

I hear the echo of laughter in my ears as she rifles through the pins on my vanity and finds the comb.

"You don't have to do this."

"I know." She begins to soothe the silken weight of my dark hair with the comb. "She won't renege on a signed contract with Maren. If you even mention it, she'll be furious."

"I know."

And Mother's fury is to be avoided at all costs.

My stomach sinks like a lead weight.

What am I going to do?

"Tell me about Etan," Andraste murmurs. "Why would marrying him be unpleasant?"

It feels strange to confide in someone, especially her. But Andraste might be my only hope. If Mother will listen to anyone, it's her.

I tell her everything, finishing with, "He said he intended to visit my tent tonight."

Andraste weaves golden chains through my hair. Little stars hang from the end of them. "If he wants to get through, then he will. He'll bribe the guards, and some of them will have overheard Mother gloating. They'll know that encouraging Aska's favor is to be allowed—"

"That's hardly reassuring—"

Our eyes meet in the mirror again as she says. "You don't have to be here."

My mouth feels dry. "Where am I going to stay?"

Staying in her tent isn't an option. The maids will gossip, and then Mother will want to know what's going on.

Andraste leans closer, resting her chin on my shoulder as she examines the masterpiece she's made of my hair. "I don't know if you can avoid this fate, Vi. I'll help you. I'll try to speak to Mother, but you know how she gets. My influence is limited, at best."

And you don't want to lose your precious seat at her side.

I look away.

"But maybe you don't have to give him everything. Etan likes your innocence, and all men like to know they're the first—maybe they're afraid they won't be able to hold up to the memory of any others? But you don't have to give it to him. Maybe you don't have the choice in who you will marry, but the gift of your virginity? That's yours to gift as you please, Vi."

"*What?*" My jaw drops open.

"*You* haven't signed the contract," she points out. "As far as Mother knows you are unaware of her plans, as she no doubt intended. The fires will burn for the next three nights while the queens meet. The wine will flow. The dancing will leave us all with blistered feet and sore heads. You're not expected to do anything other than be seen to be enjoying yourself."

"That's not exactly helpful."

"You want a choice?" Something dangerous beckons in her pretty blue eyes. "Then this is your chance to make that choice. If Etan wants your virginity then deny him that pleasure."

"I can't just sleep with a stranger!"

"Why not?" She gives a shrug. "That's what I do every Lammastide. This is the one night of the year where no one knows who I am. It's the one night of the year I can be… free."

It's the first time I've ever wondered if she feels the same way I do—trapped by the circumstance of our birth.

Could I do it?

Could I take a lover?

"And what happens afterward?"

Andraste's lashes smother her eyes. "I will see if I can convince Mother this alliance is not in our best interest."

Neither of us holds much hope of that. It's written all over her.

My mother rules Asturia with an iron fist. The whims of her daughters are never taken into consideration. We are pawns for her to move about at whim.

"There," she whispers, stepping back. "There's some color in your cheeks now. Get dressed. Meet us by Mother's tent. Hopefully by then, you'll have made a decision."

She leaves as I stare at myself in the mirror.

Find someone.

A shiver runs through me.

I'll need more than that if I'm to escape this trap.

Because I will never marry Etan of the Goldenhills.

Not even if I have to kill him myself.

THIAGO

"Why does she have to look so smug?" Thalia demands, glaring across the clearing at the Queen of Asturia.

Adaia sits upon a gilded throne before the bonfires, her expression cool and serene. A red velvet gown clings to her breasts and falls to the floor. Her pale shoulders are bare, the gown looped around her throat with a golden collar. Rings glitter on her fingers and a golden snake curls around her upper arm. It's far more muted than anything I've ever seen her wear, but the mask makes up for it.

Glorious red, blue and gold feathers, somewhat akin to a plucked parrot, cascade over her forehead. Her golden hair is slicked back and falls down her spine.

"Because Adaia doesn't know any other expression." My gaze hasn't shifted off my enemy since she arrived in this clearing, but there's something about the way Thalia says it that makes me glance down at my cousin. She's on edge. We're all on edge. But while my cousin might look like the sweetest member of my court, she's also the most dangerous when she wants to be. "Relax, Thalia. What is it you always say? Information is currency. Patience is its own reward. Right now, we have neither. We need a confirmed sighting of Finn, and then we can set plans into motion."

"Or I could simply walk across this clearing, draw my knife and drive it through that merciless bitch's heart," she murmurs as she lifts her wine glass to her lips and drains it.

"She doesn't have one." Alarm spikes through me. There are no knives on her that I can see, but then the mysteries of female clothing are lost on me. Apparently, there's a long-running vendetta against the lack of pockets on female clothing.

Thalia likes improvisation.

She designs her own wardrobe.

Which means she could be carrying half an arsenal in the folds of those skirts.

"What's wrong, Thi?" She knows exactly what I'm looking for. I can see it in those wicked green eyes.

"I love you and you know that. But I wouldn't even send Eris after Adaia, and she can kill anything," I point out. "You wouldn't stand a chance. Don't do something stupid."

Thalia merely smiles. "Oh, please, Thiago. If I wanted to kill the Queen of Asturia, she'd never see me coming. But I won't. Because that would prove a considerable headache for us right now. That doesn't mean I'm not going to retaliate. All I can say is that Adaia ought to be careful how much wine she drinks tonight."

I look at her sharply.

31

She taps the side of her nose, her mask obscuring the top half of her face. "Lysander might think my little legion is hardly going to win us a war, but he's wrong. Nobody looks at the demi-fey. Even if they're slipping powdered shepherd's rot into the queen's wine."

Shepherd's rot is a mushroom notorious for bursting the stomachs of sheep. It's rarely deadly for the fae, but it does cause a bout of indigestion that is extremely painful. The effects last for months too.

On one hand, if Adaia suspects us of being behind it then she'll only be more intractable than usual.

On the other hand, maybe it will improve *my* mood.

If I could bottle Thalia's rage and send her to war armed with only that, then I'd probably be holding Adaia's crown in my hands by the end of a week. Thalia takes great joy in fine silks and velvets, and indulging in honey cakes and sweet wine, but mistake her at your own peril.

"I have a better idea," I say as a hush falls over the gathering, my voice lowering. "Save it for the last night when we have Finn back. A gift, courtesy of Evernight."

Thalia grins at me and I straighten my mask.

It's subtle and molded expertly to my face, courtesy of Thalia. A hawk's sharp leather beak with velvet feathers. The cloak I wear is plain, my doublet made of crushed black velvet. Among all the glitter and glamour of the fae courts, nobody would look twice at me.

It's perfect.

"Let us all sing to the night," the herald calls, interrupting our plotting. He lifts his enormous staff and brings it down upon the flagstones in front of the bonfires. "Let us sing to the fires! Let us sing to the coming dawn!"

The three enormous bonfires that stand in the heart of the clearing tower over us. The queens of Aska, Ravenal and Asturia gather before them, prepared to light them, and the crowd hushes.

Right now, Eris and Baylor should be making a furtive foray into the Asturian encampment. I doubt they'll have much luck. Adaia will expect it. But I want more details about the way the camp is set up, and preferably a glimpse of Finn.

Just because the demi-fey say he's alive, it doesn't mean he's in a decent condition.

All Thalia can get out of them is *poison* and *iron sickness*. Watching the little demi-fey pretend to choke and fall to the ground would be humorous in other circumstances, but I really don't know what kind of condition he's in.

We could kill her, whispers the Darkness. *Look at her. It would be so easy.*

I lift my gaze to Adaia as I sip my wine, and the clearing vanishes around me as the world becomes black and white.

Death peeks over many a shoulder here. It would be disconcerting to see if I wasn't in the grip of the daemon within me. I am empty and hollow and my heart stills like a stone sinking to the bottom of a rushing river.

It doesn't have to beat for a heart is what stirs life through a fae's veins, and I am nothing more than Death right now.

It's quiet here in the Shadow World.

Hungry faces leer at me, superimposed over the fae beneath them. Shadows writhe as they thicken and solidify. Shadowy arms slide up a young woman's body. Dozens of them. Threatening to drag her back into her own silhouette.

She'll die soon.

Days at best. Maybe a week.

But it's Adaia who I focus on.

Adaia Thornborn.

Even in the Between, the light of her magic and power burns bright. Shadows writhe as her light pours over them, desperate to touch her and drag her down. She doesn't even know they're there.

It's a simple flex of power. I twitch my fingers and they crawl up her skirts, dragging themselves claw by claw. The light shreds, dissipating around her like smoke. The shadows are hungry. So fucking hungry.

A rushing sound fills my ears.

Hunt, whispers a voice in my head and this time it's not my daemon. It's the Darkyn soul trapped within me that I've named Fury.

Torment is not far behind it. *Gods, she tastes so divine. I want to eat her all up.*

Make her scream. Make her bleed. Crush her bones. Crunch, crunch. Rage pushes against the wards tattooed into my skin.

It feels like a knife dragging over the inside of my chest. They want out. They always want out. They're mere remnants of a whole and combined they'll form a single entity, but over the centuries, the separation has fused them into individual beings.

Adaia looks down as if she senses something. Her light dims. Her face pales and stands sallow against the flickering torches behind her.

Behind her, a shadow drags the claw of its thumb across her throat and Adaia gasps as if she feels it, clapping a hand to the mark.

"Thi?" A hand grips my arm, wrenching me back out of the gloom.

Light and heat and sound burst in upon me. For a second, it's more than I can handle and my grip tightens around the golden goblet I bear, crushing the imprint of my fingertips into it. I can barely see for the sudden brightness. Pain almost brings me to my knees; my heart, starting to beat again.

"Ignore her." There's a certain urgency in Thalia's voice.

"Weren't you the one arguing for murder?" The words sound so distant it's a wonder they came from my mouth. I blink again.

Light. Fuck, I need the light.

Claws screech down the inside of my skin like nails on a chalkboard as the daemons retreat.

"Your skin is freezing." Thalia searches my face. "What's going on?"

"Nothing."

Adaia smirks at me as she lifts her hands, her rings gleaming in the light of the torches that line the clearing. She will never know how close she came to dying this night.

Sweat breaks out upon my brow. It's never been this hard to control.

What is wrong with me?

Almost as if thinking of him summons his attention, I feel my father turn to look at me from the north. I won't

35

give him the satisfaction of responding, but I can sense his focus sliding over my skin like the pad of a finger trailing down a long-bleached spine.

Searching for me. Yearning to destroy me. To consume me.

Wondering perhaps, who it is that catches his attention every now and then.

He's never seen me. He doesn't even know I exist.

But he can sense me—or the daemon inside him can.

It's inside me too, and it yearns to be whole.

Thousands of years ago it stalked these lands. Death, they called it. The Everlasting Night. The Primordial Darkness. A creature so malevolent and powerful that even the Old Ones feared it.

A band of fae warriors spent their entire lives hunting it, and when they finally captured it, they had to consume fragments of its body and soul in order to defeat it. It cannot die. It cannot be contained. They were forced to venture to the ends of the world in order to separate its desperate soul, and I wonder if those long ago fae felt the crush of this hunger, this need, this yearning to reunite.

Somewhere along the way, some of them fell prey to its lure.

They hunted their own, consuming the fragments of that Darkness.

Now only a few of us remain.

My father, who birthed this evil within me, and myself, veiled and cloaked from his eyes with the best illusions any fae can wield. There are two others, I think, somewhere far to the west and east, but I suspect a sea stands between us for I can rarely feel them.

Of the five Darkyn souls trapped within me, only two of them ever give me any peace.

Thalia slides her fingers through mine, and I relish every inch of heat within her.

"As the days turn, we celebrate the end of harvest and the beginning of the long chill," Lucidia of Ravenal calls as she slowly pushes to her feet and moves toward the torch that awaits her.

Tonight the Veil begins to thin between worlds, and will not strengthen until the third night. Pocket realms may open. Strange creatures sometimes slip between worlds. In the ancient days, before the fae locked the Old Ones in their prison worlds, they hunted nights like this.

"As the Veil thins," calls Maren of Aska, lifting her torch, "we light the fires to protect against the night. We bring praise for the light. We ask for protection from Blessed Maia."

"As the night falls," Adaia says as she steps forward, fire spinning to life in her hands, her skin brightening as if she's shaken off my shadows, "we three queens offer our protection against all of those who hold wicked and sinister thoughts in their hearts. We three queens offer protection, light and strength. Blessed be."

"Blessed be," echo Lucidia and Maren.

The other two set their torches to their bonfires, but Adaia waves her hand and flames shoot up in the dry kindling, consuming it like a blazing inferno.

Power. Light. Protection.

It makes for a flamboyant show and she's reveling in this moment.

I exchange a glance with Prince Kyrian of Stormlight

from across the clearing. He offers me a faint smile and an arched brow. Adaia couldn't have been blunter if she'd tried—in her mind, both Kyrian and I are an abomination, an unnatural blight on the Seelie world.

Queens rule.

The line of power is passed through the matrilineal line.

And if she had her way, she would crush us back into the swamps she suggests we both come from.

We three queens.

Indeed.

Cheers erupt through the gathered fae as the bonfires roar. Music strikes up; a merry jig. And then a host of the fae are being swept onto the grassy plain before the fires.

It's like a discordant note against my soul. I'm still cold. Still distant.

I need to get moving to force the blood through my starved veins.

"Where are you going?" Thalia asks as she darts in my path. "Don't you dare simply vanish. We're supposed to be waiting for the princess of Ravenal."

"I need a moment."

"Just dance with Princess Lucere, Thiago. Once." Thalia's eyes promise murder if I ruin her plans. "Talk to her. That's all we've promised. You may like her."

This was the price I promised to pay all those years ago when I took the throne. Anything for my people. Anything for my mother's kingdom.

Anything for those who serve me.

"Thalia." *Just give me a fucking moment.*

Her face brightens into a wide smile. "Here they come.

Paste a smile on your face. Picture Adaia sipping on shepherd's rot, if that helps. Be smooth. Be charming." She gives me a look. "I know you have it in you."

Too late to make an escape. I square my shoulders. So be it. Let's get this over with.

But my steps are slow, my heart like lead in my chest as I start toward the Ravenal delegation with Thalia on my arm.

They see me coming.

A young woman straightens abruptly as if she sucks in a sharp breath. She wears white from head-to-toe, and her long, raven hair is bound into a glossy mound atop her head. Not a single strand of it dares hang loose.

Regal. Beautiful. Daring.

Princess Lucere.

I swallow the hard lump in my throat and force a smile to my lips. "She looks like an ice princess."

"She's... reserved," Thalia admits.

"And how are you all going to get along with her?" There's a camaraderie within my court that feels like home. To throw this walking icicle into their midst will dash away those careless smiles, and teasing tones.

It's my one respite.

The one place I can simply *be*.

"If you can manage, we can manage. Now, is that your best smile?"

I shake my head. She's incorrigible—

And just at that moment, the dancers part and a woman appears as if she's stepped directly from my dreams.

Her.

My breath catches in my chest and somehow I can't move.

A woman gowned in starlight. Her skirts are of the darkest blue, with diamond chips woven through the gauze so it almost seems as if she glimmers like the night sky. A silver mask gleams with gemstones, catching the light as she tilts her face to the bonfires.

It's not the dress that captures my attention.

It's not the mask.

It's not even her beauty.

It's the shape of her mouth and chin—

The same mouth that's been haunting my dreams for centuries.

I can't move. I can barely breathe.

Is it a mirage?

Is it *her*?

Is she the promise of light that Maia sent to me so long ago?

I have to know.

"Thiago?" Thalia's voice is distant behind me as I plunge through the dancers, searching for the woman of my dreams.

Nothing else matters.

4

ISKVIEN

The music takes my breath away as fae leap and dance. My mother's celebrations are hedonistic in every way, but there's something raw and powerful about the sound of that music. It sings a song of wild magic.

Light the bonfires against the ancient darkness.

Sing and dance until morning, when dawn lights the skies and we are finally safe.

Breathe, laugh, kiss. Joy will shield us from the Wild Hunt. Laughter will make the Erlking's toes tap. Music will confound his hounds, and tempt the Erlking from his hunt...

There is no Wild Hunt anymore.

There hasn't been for years, with the Erlking and his cohort locked away. He used to hunt the world on nights like these, when the Veil thins, stealing away fair maidens and youths.

But the tradition remains.

I once asked Nanny what he did with those he stole and she told me the story was not for my ears.

Though a heated blush stole through her cheeks and she leaned close and whispered, "They say what he did to them ruined them. He would steal them away for a year and a day, until the Veil next thinned. They would return from his magic court, but they were never the same. They begged to return. They found no comfort in our fae foods, no pleasure in our touch. They became hollow and empty, and could only find solace in music and dancing. But what the stories don't say is that foolish young maidens ventured out on those nights when the winds howled, desperate to be claimed as his tribute. Because the Erlking is everything powerful and wild, dangerous and tempting. Dance to distract him, Vi. He loves the dance. He loves our music. It's the one thing that can sway his predatory instincts."

There is no Erlking anymore but as the music sweeps me up, I can't help feeling my heart beating in my chest like a drum.

The fae part as I slip through them. I want to look everywhere at once. I don't recognize a single soul, and while I'm sure one of my mother's guards is following me, I haven't managed to mark him.

"A drink, my love?" A fae dressed as a leprechaun shoves a golden goblet into my hand and elderberry wine splashes over my wrist.

"Oh, leave her be," says his woman, slinging an arm around his neck as she looks me up and down. "Unless you want to join us?"

There's no doubt what she's suggesting. The forest is woven with lanterns and there are numerous little bowers out there in the woods, decorated with berries and sheaves of wheat—for fertility. I wave them away, thanking him for the drink.

It's at that moment that I sense someone watching me.

It's a prickling sensation down my spine. A languid caress.

Sipping at the wine I search the clearing, but there's only laughter and dancing. A fae lordling draws a woman into his lap as another kisses her shoulder. A garishly painted woman swallows an entire flaming sword. Dozens of gorgeous fae maids are swung into the air as the fiddle kicks in.

The wine glides down my throat, but it doesn't mask the sensation I'm being watched.

But who?

Night-blooming flowers suddenly burst to life in the sky.

Someone's hired an enchanter to paint the night bright, and the *crack* and *pop* of sound makes me shiver.

A golden head appears between two dancers, a male wearing a lion's mask. I'd recognize those broad shoulders anywhere.

Etan.

And he's looking for someone.

Me, if I was to place any coin on it. He's already claimed my dances. And Mother insisted I allow it.

Gods, it wasn't someone's eyes upon me that I was sensing, but danger in itself. If he sees me then I'll be forced to dance with him, and right now, I'm still furious enough at my mother's demands that I don't know if I can bite down on my words.

I turn, desperate to escape, and it feels as though the crowd in front of me parts at my whim.

They're not parting for me.

Too late, I realize there's a tide of darkness swimming toward me. A wolf prowling through the dancers, forcing them to yield to him. He's shockingly tall, clad in leather and black velvet. His short hair is the color of sable, his skin a healthy olive. Unlike the rest of the fae, there's not a single glittering ring or bead upon him. Just cold, merciless black.

But there's nothing cold about the look on his face. Nothing merciless about his expression. Only... intensity. Our gazes lock and it feels like time stands still.

The world vanishes.

The music fades.

It's like we stepped sideways into another world where only the two of us exist. And maybe it's true. Maybe the Veil thinned in this precise moment.

Is he an ancient god brought to life?

Did I conjure the Erlking with my thoughts?

No. No. If anything, this male is far too mortal to be the Erlking. There's a vitality to the Erlking, all the stories say. But this male is... a little too coldly lethal. The music flows over him as if he doesn't hear it. He radiates strength and determination, his focus locked entirely upon me. Or maybe that's the mask that decorates his upper face.

A hawk.

A hawk that's caught its prey.

My heart flutters in my chest. I can't breathe.

I don't even know why.

"Dance with me," he says, offering his arm and finally

smiling. If the Erlking does exist, then he sounds exactly like this: firm and commanding, the slightest hint of wickedness rolling through his words.

He's much bigger than he seemed across the clearing. Broad shoulders. Hard muscle. All of it hidden beneath the refined cut of his doublet. Despite the lack of jewelry, I recognize good tailoring when I see it and this is exquisite. Every inch of his clothing caresses his body like a second skin. He oozes sophisticated elegance, but there's a hint of danger smoldering beneath the surface.

"Do I have a choice?" I can't help being on the offensive; he's just a little too overwhelming.

"You always have a choice." Taking my hand he lifts it to his lips. "Me? Not so. Fate took me by the heart five centuries ago and tattooed you there on my soul."

A nervous shiver runs through me as his lips brush against my knuckles.

I can feel his breath.

Feel the heat of him.

"A very practiced line," I point out.

He laughs a little, almost at himself. "If only you knew the truth."

"Iskvien?" The sound echoes across the clearing.

Etan's finally found me and though dozens of dancers separate us, he's visibly seething as he sees my hand clasped in this stranger's grip.

Alarm kicks through me.

I have to go.

"Forgive me—"

My stranger catches a fistful of my skirt and I can almost see the unspoken command in his eyes.

Stay.

The word tremors through me, even as our eyes meet.

"Dance with me," he repeats.

This is a terrible idea. Etan is pushing through the crowd toward us—I can't even tear my eyes from the stranger's face to see where my nemesis is, but I saw Etan start this way.

I don't even know his name. His court. Who he belongs to.

There's no answer in the unrelenting black of his clothing. Black and silver are the colors of Evernight, of course, but no lord of Evernight would ever approach *me*. And there are enough black-clad strangers here that the color alone doesn't make him stand out.

"I shouldn't."

Finally, a smile blooms on that dangerous mouth. "No. You shouldn't. I shouldn't. But the second I saw you I had to know you. What's your name?"

"As if I'm going to hand some handsome stranger my name."

His lips curl upwards. "You think me handsome?"

"You know you're handsome." I push at him, snatching a glance behind me.

It's like trying to shift a mountain.

"Who is he?" The stranger demands, and tension coils through him.

"You want to dance with me?" I blurt. "Then get me out of here. Get me as far away from him as you can and I will grant you a dance. I will grant you a dozen of them."

Stillness.

"I'll hold you to that," my stranger breathes. "But as you wish…."

He swings his cloak over me, tucking me under his shoulder and the world vanishes, the dancers and the music dropping away. It's like we took a step between this world and another.

I can see ghosts of the others still moving. Wisps of a skirt appearing here and there. Laughter ringing out before it cuts off.

My handsome stranger sweeps me into the crowd, an arm draped around my hips. A spin, and suddenly we're in the middle of the dancefloor. I catch a glimpse of the back of Etan's head, barely a foot away as he searches for us.

And then we're gone again.

A guard I recognize as my mother's appears, up on his toes as he scans the crowd. They're all here. They're all looking for me. There's some kind of illicit thrill in stealing away from both of them.

A hop, a skip, a twirl.

It feels like I'm spinning in circles.

The stranger lets me go as I stagger into the trees, his cloak falling from my shoulders. Music hammers at me, drums vibrating through the trees. The fae are back, no longer mere hints of movement.

I press my spine to the ivy-covered tree, my eyes darting over his shoulder. Etan's expression tightens with anger when he clearly can't find me.

"Forget about him," my handsome stranger whispers.

"I'm trying."

Something soft brushes over her lip. "Does this help?"

It's his thumb, tracing my lower lip so slowly that a fist of heat knots between my thighs.

Our eyes meet.

And then the back of his knuckles ripple over my jaw. He makes a small sound in his throat as if he finds the contours of my face fascinating.

A shiver runs through me. There's barely an inch between us, as if he's trying to give me just enough space that I don't feel caged.

"What was that? How did you do that?"

He takes my hand in his, that dangerous smile back in place. "Magic, my love."

I eye his cloak. "I need to get one of those."

He laughs, and the sound catches somewhere in my chest as if some part of me knows it's not a sound the world hears very often. "It's not the cloak, princess."

I can't help stilling. *Princess.* "I wouldn't dare claim such a title."

"Not yet, anyway," he says mysteriously, and then he tugs at my fingertips. "Let us leave this clearing far behind. You owe me a dozen dances anyway…."

"And so you intend to claim them?"

"Oh, yes." There's a look in his eyes that brands me. "I intend to claim them all."

"That's somewhat presumptuous of you."

He pauses, one arm extended as he gestures for me to follow him. "Come with me. Dance with me. *Please.*"

I run my tongue over my teeth. There's something about him that intrigues me.

And Maia knows I've spent enough years dancing to

my mother's tune. This time, it's my *choice* whether to take this risk or not.

And I want it.

I want to take his hand. I want to dance with him. Maybe steal a kiss. He's wickedly handsome, after all.

Maybe steal something… more?

Heat works through me again. I've played by the rules all my life, and this is where it's gotten me.

I slowly release a breath and clasp our hands together. "Then I will."

THE CELEBRATIONS SPILL FROM ONE CLEARING TO ANOTHER. The music shifts and changes. My dark stranger sweeps me into a jig, and then a reel, and then something slower.

It's the *something slower* that makes me feel nervous.

His body is carved of hot sin, his eyes like smoke and thunder. He whirls me under his arm, again and again and again, until I'm dancing on the tip of my toes, my skirts flying around us. I come back into his arms, breathless with the sensation of his body against mine.

"I think I have paid you your quota of dances."

"True. I thought perhaps to earn more."

"Earn more? And how would you do that?" I tease.

"Come," he whispers in my ear as the music lulls. "Why don't we go somewhere private?"

You want a choice? Andraste whispers in my memories. *Then this is your chance to make that choice.*

"I don't know if I trust you or not."

49

He stills. "I would never hurt you."

Of course not. They all say that. I press a hand to his chest. "As lovely as that sounds, you *are* asking me to disappear into the woods with you. I don't know who you are. I don't know what you intend...."

"I intend to get to know you."

"I'm sure you do."

Another heated look. "I only intend to get to know you." His smile is wicked. "I don't let myself get lured into the woods by women when I don't even know their name."

I bite my lip and shake my head. "Best if you don't know."

"But if I don't know, then how am I going to find you again?" His eyes search my soul.

"Vi." It blurts from my lips and I nearly stifle a moan. I can't believe I just betrayed myself like that.

"*Vi*." There's something about the way he says the word that undoes me.

"For V-Violet." I look him in the eye. What's the harm in this one little lie? He'll never know. Tomorrow will come and I'll vanish like the figment of a dream.

He looks a little disappointed when I don't ask him the same.

And then he slips his mask from his face.

My breath catches. Again. I knew he was handsome, but I didn't realize just how much. There's a dangerous carnality to him. Green eyes. He has green eyes. They're the color of a forest cat's and just as predatory. Thick dark brows and silky lashes complete the look.

It's like he strips away this layer deliberately.

See me. Know me.

And then he lifts his hand to my face. "May I?"

We're in the shadows of the trees, but there are other dancers close behind us and my face is not unknown.

I take his fingers and plunge us into the forest. "Not yet. I still haven't decided if I'm going to let you do this."

"You're the one leading me into parts unknown," he teases. "Maybe I should be afraid for *my* virtue?"

It's safer here. No eyes to see us. No ears to hear us.

I pause, with my back to a nearby tree. "I… find it difficult to trust."

He searches my face again. Nods. And then he goes to one knee. "Then I grant you control over me for this one night. Command me, my fair lady. I bind myself to your whims. I promise once, I promise twice, I promise thrice— whatever you ask of me until the dawn rises, I am bound to give you."

He *can't* be serious.

The fae are bound by their oaths and this effectively gives me control over him. If I asked him to kill someone, then he *must* do it.

"What are you doing?" I take a step back. "What if I asked you to do something you're not comfortable doing?"

"You won't." There's not even a single hint of doubt on his face. "You don't trust me, Vi, so this grants you the power between us." A slight pause. "You won't hurt me. You won't ask of me anything I don't wish to do. I have faith in that."

To see him like this on one knee before me—

"Get up."

He pushes to his feet and I clap my hands over my mouth. His eyes are twinkling as he sees my dilemma.

I push away from him. It feels overwhelming. I've never had such power and now it lies in my hand, it's a horrifying burden. Every word I speak must be carefully chosen.

"Come," he whispers, extending his hand. "You're safe now. Because now I *can't* hurt you. There's a place by the lake that I would like to show you. The views are spectacular."

And it's no doubt private.

I look down at those gloved fingers.

I don't even know what's come over me as I place my hand over those leather-clad fingers. "Okay," I whisper.

THE SMALL OUTCROPPING OF STONE BY THE LAKE JUTS A little higher than everything else.

We're so far away from the rites that it seems like a dream. Lights glow through the forest below, and music comes in drifts of the wind. On the lake, the stars dance across those dark waters and I look up to see them shining brilliantly in the sky.

"It's beautiful," I whisper.

I can't help thinking that I'm safe up here, so far away from Etan that he'll never find me.

"Truly," my handsome stranger breathes, and there's a reverence to his voice that makes me seek him out. His eyes are on my face but he remains seated on a boulder, giving me enough space to feel comfortable.

"I don't know why you're doing this," I blurt.

He smiles, leaning back on his hands. "Doing what?"

"You could have danced with dozens of others—"

"I only wanted to dance with you."

"But *why*?"

This time, he's the one who looks away. "Do you believe in fate, Vi?"

A shiver runs down my spine. "I believe in the gods. I believe in… in magic. I believe we are driven by our own choices. But fate? I think fate is what you make of it."

There's something ancient in his eyes as he stares back at me. "I believe in fate. I believe I was meant to meet you this one night. It feels like the world has been holding its breath forever and the second I saw you, it finally exhaled. You and I—this night—was meant to be."

"I think you've been drinking too much of the elder-berry wine."

He laughs. "You don't believe in fate and I do. Let us agree upon this then—if fate is what you make of it, then what are we to make of this? This *chance* encounter."

It's a heady feeling. If fate is what we make of it, then what *do* I wish for? He's a stranger. I don't even know what I'm doing with him. Or why. But I can't deny there's something intriguing about him.

"What do you want to make of it?" I ask.

Dark lashes flutter over his eyes. "I would like to kiss you. Just once. To see if fate has been telling me the truth."

"And what truth would that be?"

"That this kiss was written in the stars."

I step closer, between his thighs. "Do you know what I think?"

"What?" He tilts his face back to look up at me. It's barely an inch in difference, but it makes me feel powerful.

53

"I think you would have made an excellent courtier."

His teeth flash white in the night. "Maybe I am one."

"Maybe." I press my finger against his lips. "No. Don't tell me. It would ruin this."

It's easier if I don't know who he is, because then I don't have to pretend. I don't have to think of politics or alliances. It doesn't become a bad idea, a regret. It simply stays as it is….

A harmless, slightly-flirtatious encounter with a dark stranger on a moonlit night.

"Ruin this?" Reaching up slowly, he tries for my mask again. "I want to see you."

I don't know why but the simple act of removing my mask feels like he's stripping me to the skin.

"Stop panicking," he says.

"I'm not panicking."

"No?" There's a teasing light in his eyes and his finger-tips graze my cheeks. "All you have to do is say one little word, Vi, and I am bound to obey you."

"I don't like this bargain." The mask slips from my skin. "I don't like holding your fate in my hands. I can't believe you made that promise."

"Maybe it was a test." He lowers the mask.

He looks at me as if I'm beautiful, as if he's trying to memorize the fine lines of my face. His eyes flare wide, drinking me in.

It's such a vulnerable moment. I've never been beauti-ful. Not at my mother's court.

"A test?"

"You passed," he whispers. "If you weren't concerned

about the situation, then you wouldn't be the woman I want you to be."

I can't help thinking.... "Do you do this every Lammastide? Throw yourself upon the mercy of a stranger?"

"Always." And then he laughs. "Never. I've never wanted a woman like this."

"Stop it," I whisper.

"Stop what?"

"Stop looking at me like that. Stop looking at me as if I'm beautiful. I'm not. I know I'm not and I'm fine with it—"

He lifts a hand, brushing that gloved thumb down my cheek. "Who told you such nonsense?"

"I have seen the women of my court. I don't compare—"

"You don't compare yourself to other fae, Vi. Because I have never seen one such as you. Compare yourself to the stars and dare them to shine half as bright." His fingertips rest on either side of my face. "You were made for the night. You were made for moonlight and stolen kisses." His thumb brushes against my lips. "This mouth was made for secrets. It was made for me."

A skittering breath escapes me. "You're good."

He leans closer and my heart erupts. "I speak only the truth. Maybe I am the night. Maybe you were made just for me. Maybe you're perfect as you are."

Our breaths mingle. I don't even know how he's done it—slipped through my defenses while I wasn't looking. He's a stranger. I should be on guard. But here he is, his thumbs stroking my mouth so gently I want to let him kiss me.

But he doesn't.

"You would have to command me," he murmurs as if he can sense what I'm thinking. "I will not take what is not freely given. Command me, Vi. Tell me to kiss you."

My heart flutters like a captured butterfly. *Find a stranger.... Take what you want from him....* I never dreamed this would actually be happening. I never thought for a second that there might be someone out there tonight who would tempt me to push past my natural reticence.

A shiver runs through me. He's so patient, merely waiting for me to make this decision. *Yes* or *no*? It's in his eyes.

But what is in my heart?

"Kiss me." The words are out before I can stop them. "Just a kiss."

"As you wish."

His hand slides through my hair, cupping the back of my nape and then he draws me into his arms. My heart skips a beat as his lips brush against mine. He's not the first male I've ever kissed. But he *feels* like the first. Because he doesn't simply grab me and maul me.

His lips whisper over mine as if they're saying "Hello."

Back and forth. There's a luxurious kind of gentleness to him, as if he's got all the time in the world to taste me, and so he wants to do this right. It's the kind of kiss a first kiss should be.

My hands find the crushed velvet of his doublet. I was right. Every inch of him is hard steel beneath the fine clothes and my fists curl into his collar as I press into him. I want that mouth. I want him to *kiss* me.

But he's made it clear that my consent matters. It's me who opens to him first, tracing my tongue against his lower lip in a silent demand.

A soft laugh echoes through his chest. "So be it."

Everything changes.

Pushing to his feet, he claims my mouth.

I'm not so unschooled with kissing that I don't know what I'm doing, but when his tongue brushes against mine, I can't help drawing back with a sharp gasp. This is madness.

His mouth is a hungry demand. My thighs bump against the rock behind me and I'm caged between his body and the outcropping. One hand slides down my spine, curling into my bottom. I gasp as he squeezes there, grinding me up against him. My nipples go hard as his tongue lashes against mine. It's heady. Overwhelming. I've spent a lifetime listening to the poets at court speak of the desperation a single kiss can conjure, but I've never felt it before.

This is desperation.

I can't control the want, the sheer need within me. Maybe it's because this is forbidden that I tremble so. Maybe it's because there's an underlying hint of danger to the scenario. He's a stranger. Gentle. Kind. Dangerous.

This is so, so dangerous.

And I don't care.

A groan rumbles through his chest. "Easy, easy."

I slide my arms around his neck and kiss him hard, chasing pleasure off his lips. All the things I've wanted to do to him since I first laid eyes upon him are mine to do.... Hands brush like feather strokes down my waist as if he's trying to gentle me, but his mouth doesn't retreat. He wants this as much as I do. I can feel the tremor running through him, and then there's barely any space between us as he thrusts against me.

Something hard nudges against my hip. Despite my determination, I steal a gasp. It's a shock to know him in such a way.

"Vi." He breathes the word against my lips, capturing my face again. "Vi, wait."

I don't want him to stop.

I want his hands to keep moving, to take away my last remaining doubts. I want him to coax me and seduce me, convince me to keep going....

But he doesn't, of course.

Drawing back, he rests his forehead against mine as I tremble against him. We're both panting. I want more. I want to slide my hands beneath his clothes and find the heated silk of his skin. I want to run my teeth over the corded muscle in his throat.

But he captures my wrists and presses a gentle kiss to each of my knuckles.

"Patience, my love. Patience. Talk to me." He laughs again. "Or maybe I just need a moment. You take all my good intentions and throw them to the wind."

"What do you want to talk about?"

His smile is dangerous. "Do you believe in fate now?"

A kiss that was written in the stars....

Despite myself, I shiver. "Maybe I would believe in fate if it wasn't currently trying to slow this down."

He laughs.

And then he nuzzles against my throat, holding me as if we're dancing slowly together to some music neither of us can hear. "I think I want to keep kissing you. Forever." A shudder runs through him. "But... that can wait. It can all wait. Tell me about yourself. I want to know everything."

Tension dissolves like acid in my chest. The second I mention my mother's name, his smile will slide off his face as if it never existed. "I'm not very interesting."

"Am I not to be the judge of that?"

"Maybe I want to remain a woman of mystery."

Thoughtful, smoldering eyes examine every inch of my face as he draws back. I can't tell what he's thinking. But he can sense my withdrawal.

"We could be enemies," I point out swiftly as I tug free of his hands. "There are five courts here and I know I've never seen you before."

Which means he's not from Aska. If *he'd* been stalking the hallways of the castle there, then I would never have even looked at Etan.

He's not Asturian. He's not Askan. My heart skips a beat. There are only three kingdoms remaining: Ravenal, Stormlight... and Evernight.

The first two leave me breathless with hope, but it's the last one that steals my breath.

The Prince of Evernight is a monster and I daresay his violent tendencies would rub off on his court. That's what princes like him do—they gather those around them who thrive on their cruelty, and turn a blind eye to their monstrosities.

He can't be from Evernight. I'm sure of that.

And even if he *is* from Stormlight, that's not so… unpalatable. Is it?

"Are you sure about that?" There's a teasing lilt to his voice.

"I'd remember."

There's a strange freedom in this moment. He doesn't know who I am. I could be anyone. I could be anything I wanted to be. I don't have to be Iskvien, the daughter of a vicious queen.

"It doesn't matter who we are, or which court we belong to," he finally says. "Not tonight."

"Good." I grab his hand and press it to my heart. "I want you to…. I want it to be you." I swiftly correct my words. "I want you to lie with me. Tonight."

There's a heated look in his eyes and seconds trip out, until I can barely stomach the tension. *Say yes. Please say yes….*

"I shouldn't," he whispers, reaching up and running the back of his fingers through my hair. "I should wait. I should woo you."

I don't have time for any of that.

I nip at his fingers, and the doubt that's in his eyes is replaced with heat.

"But you present a convincing argument." He kisses my throat. His voice roughens. "I want you. I want you under me. I want my mouth all over you. Give me a command, my love. Tell me what you want of me."

"I don't want you to do anything you don't want to do."

He takes in a slow breath. "Believe me, my love. You

couldn't—"

I press a finger to his lips. "Promise or no promise, if I ask of you something you don't wish to do, you must tell me no."

Those eyes become dark pools. "I promise."

Good. It takes away any doubts I own. I've been trapped in a cage for so long that I want to revel in every moment of this. I want to take this moment and claim it for my own. I crave it. Crave his touch, crave the experience of this moment.

It's no longer just about denying Etan.

It's no longer about defying my mother.

This is for me.

It's the gift I want for myself. It's the choice *I* make.

I want to know what it feels like to be touched. I want to know what it feels like to come under his hands and mouth. I want him to fuck me into this heather, until I'm screaming.

I want it all.

"Lie down." There's a strength to the words that I barely even recognize.

A challenge lights in his eyes, but he obeys.

Silvery light falls over us as he reclines on his elbows in the heather, his enormous chest rising and falling with each desperate breath he takes. "I feel a little like a blushing virgin. Should I disrobe? Are you planning on seducing me, my love?"

He keeps calling me that.

"Always," I whisper. My heart trips all over itself as I reach behind my neck and draw the ribbons on my dress loose. Instantly, the fabric of my bodice loosens, my nipples furling into tight buds behind the silk. His eyes darken, his breath catching in his chest as if he didn't expect this. Maybe that's what gives me the strength of will to do this. The dress slides down my skin, pooling around my feet.

There's nothing beneath the dress.

Nothing but my heart slamming against my ribs as I stand bare before him.

"*Maia's breath*," he whispers in awe. "What are you doing to me?"

"Aren't we playing at blushing virgin and reckless rogue?" It's easier to tease him and pretend I'm not so vulnerable.

"We are." He bites his bottom lip. "I'm just not sure if I should let you have my innocence. I barely know you. You might be planning to ruin me."

"Oh, I plan on ruining you." I can't help laughing.

He shakes his head. "This is not what I intended when I first saw you."

"You're such a liar," I say, pulling pins from my hair and letting my hair fall in silken tangles over my shoulders. "Show me what you would do to a woman on a night like this. Show me what happens when you steal her away from the bonfires."

My handsome stranger stares up at me, every inch of him arrested.

And then he sits up, reaching over his shoulder to haul his doublet off. Muscle curls in his abdominals. I see the ripple of them, before he's casting his clothing aside.

He holds out a hand. "Then come here. And I will show you."

5

THIAGO

G ods, she's so fucking perfect as she slides into my lap and presses her lips to mine.

All these years and she's finally here in my arms. I can't stop kissing her. I can't stop tracing my palms over her skin. She's real. She's here.

She's mine.

I had plans for the evening the second I saw her. She would be skittish. I needed to get to know her, woo her, gods, maybe even kiss her....

But she destroyed those plans the second she kissed me.

The moment she stripped off that gown all my thoughts of a slow seduction dissolved like a dream. She doesn't want to know my name, or where I come from. She just wants this. *Fine*. I can work with that. I will have her one way or the other.

"Now what?" I ask, brushing my hand up her thigh as our lips break apart. Her skin is like silk.

"I don't know." There's a hint of a blush to her cheeks.

"*You're* ruining *me*," I point out.

"Yes, but…. I've never been in this position before." Her gaze drops away. "I don't chase strange males. I don't kiss them. I don't…. I don't do this."

I take pity on her. "This?"

Taking her hand I place her palms on my chest and glide them over my skin. Her breath catches, her gaze focusing on what her hands are doing. It gives me a moment to examine her face.

Gods, I've dreamed of her thousands of times, imagined her thousands more, but I never even came close to the truth. There's a certain type of wonder in her expression, as if she's inexperienced. I doubt that's the truth. She wouldn't have simply stripped her gown off if she was— and she's clearly after pleasure tonight and nothing else— but it makes an odd shiver run through my gut.

Mine. She feels like mine in all the ways that matter. My cock aches. I want to roll her onto her back and drive myself into her. I want it so desperately I can barely restrain myself.

But I do.

I capture those wrists and lift one of her hands to my mouth, pressing a gentle kiss to her palm. Our eyes meet. She shivers. And only then do I let myself look at the rest of her.

She's lean and lightly muscled. No delicate court lady, this one. The sleek muscles in her thighs argue for hours in the saddle, and the clear delineation in her arms speaks of some form of manual labor. There's a faint callus on her hand too. I capture it and explore that callus, forced to seek my answers in her skin since she's so unforthcoming.

I have answering calluses on my own hands, though mine are on both palms.

Sword work?

How intriguing. She doesn't bear the form of a warrior, nor a guard, but someone's taught her about footwork. I could see it while we danced. She's not merely trained in the art of dancing—though her form there *is* excellent. It's more than that.

So she dances like a court-trained lady. She clearly knows her way around a sword. And the stables.

Aristocrat, my mind supplies, but probably not of the highest echelons. She doesn't speak like a woman who is used to commanding others. She doesn't like knowing she has me at her mercy tonight. She's too *kind* to be a member of some ruling family somewhere.

"You're beautiful," she whispers, tracing the "tattoos" across my chest.

I feel Wrath stirring against her touch, and force him deep inside. Capturing her hand, I kiss it again. "You keep stealing all my lines, my love."

"Mmm. What next?" she whispers. "If I were seducing you, what would I do next?"

I kiss my way up the inside of her arm, flexing upright, until she sinks into the cradle of my hips. "You would grab a fistful of my hair," I whisper, "and let me taste those beautiful breasts."

She complies immediately and I shudder as she brings my face to her skin. I'm not the only one. The second my mouth closes over her nipple, she gasps and grinds against me. *Fuck.* She's so responsive. I suckle hard, even as she rocks against me instinctively. I'm

65

ridiculously close to spending in my trousers. I haven't been this on edge since I was a young fae warrior in his prime.

Capturing her in my arms, I roll her onto her back, tracing my tongue around and around her nipple. Our eyes meet as she moans.

I could drown in her eyes. They're a starry night, an endless canvas of the darkest midnight. I can't hold back any longer. I drive up and capture that dangerous mouth, the one that's causing me to lose control, lose all my focus.

She kisses me back exuberantly, twining her arms around my neck.

There's something about the way she kisses that steals my breath.

Holding nothing back. Giving everything of herself and more. There's no artifice in her. No games. Nothing beyond need. She kisses me as if she needs my mouth the way she needs oxygen.

"Vi." I breathe the word against her throat. "You're getting dangerously close to undoing me."

"Good," she purrs. "Why don't you undo those trousers?"

"Is that a command?"

"Does it need to be?"

"I don't know. You're the one in control."

She drags her fingernails down my chest. "Then take them off. Take it all off. I want to see you bare."

I rear onto my knees, my hands dropping to my buttons. Her gaze follows my fingers and so I make it a tease. One button at a time, until I'm fisting the hard shaft of my erection. The way she looks at me....

"You're… huge." Her eyes widen, and she brushes tentative fingers against me.

Capturing her hand, I curl her fingers around me. "You say all the right things," I tease. "Are you sure I'm not the first stranger you've lured into the darkness?"

"Fairly certain." There's a wicked glint in her eyes.

I slowly stroke her hand up and down my length. My nostrils flare. I'm not going to last long if we continue this. And as much as I love the feel of her hands on my skin, I want my mouth on hers.

Reaching out, I trail my hand down her abdomen. A shiver runs through her as I reach the thatch of hair between her thighs. She grows very still.

"I want to kiss you. Right here." I delve my fingertips into that wetness and she gasps.

"Then do it," she blurts.

I kiss my way up her thighs as she lies back. Tension coils within her as I nuzzle into soft, wet flesh. She's so fucking delicious. A soft cry greets me as I lick her in slow, deep strokes, gazing up the length of her body. Hands sink into my hair. It's a silent entreaty.

A silent command.

As my lady wishes….

Flicking my tongue against her, I chase after each and every shiver. Restless gasps tear from her lips.

"You're so fucking wet." I love it. I want more. Capturing her ass in both my hands I drive my face into her, licking and tonguing her deep. Torturing her with soft, teasing strokes, before returning to shove my tongue into her.

She cries out in shock, grinding herself against my

face. I love the taste of her, the little tremor of aftershocks that run through her. The way she begs for more….

I want her to beg for mercy. I want her on her hands and knees before me, her arms bound behind her back, and her face pressing into my mattress as I fuck her hard….

It's not my thoughts.

It's not me.

Or not the me I want to be. I shudder into her pussy.

Fuck her, whispers my Darkness. *Take her. Claim her as ours. Don't ever let her go….*

I force it all down by focusing on her. Control is the altar I worship at. I will lock this beast away inside me where it can never, ever get out.

I haven't lost control in five hundred years. I won't start now.

"Oh, gods." Her spine arches like a bow and then she's hovering there, right on the edge of the storm.

I slide a finger inside her tight sheathe, stroking up, curling against that delicate little patch inside her.

She shatters with a tortured scream and I ride her through it, hungry for every gasp and breathy demand. And then she's collapsing beneath me, shaking and over-sensitive. Mine to kiss. Mine to claim.

Simply mine.

"Mmm." I press a kiss against her thigh. "I could do that all night."

"I can't." A fist tangles in my hair. "I want you. *Please.* I want you. Now."

No more denying myself. Or her. I surge upright, fisting my cock. Five hundred years of waiting for her. I don't have to wait anymore. I want her so desperately I can barely control myself.

"How do you want it?" I gasp, as I settle between her thighs. "Hard? Or slow?"

She melts beneath me with a gasp as I trace the head of my cock through her wetness. Nails dig into my upper arms. "Just. *Now.*"

So be it.

Capturing her mouth, I drive into her in one slow thrust—

And she cries out, her body locking so tight around me it feels like a glove, a vise. Every inch of me goes still. No. *No.* But it's there in every moment of our encounter.

Her hesitancy. Her curiosity.

The way her flesh gripped my finger.

If I were seducing you, what would I do next?

I am such a fucking idiot.

"Vi?" I whisper, because I can't believe I've done this. All these years of waiting for her, and I didn't even ask if she was experienced or not. "Are you a virgin?"

She takes a deep breath, stroking the muscle in my upper arm as she shudders beneath me. "I think that's... in the past tense now."

There's a rushing, roaring sound in my ears. "Why didn't you tell me?"

"Because it didn't matter." She bites her lip. "I wanted it to be you. I just want this one night with you."

One night is never going to be enough.

And if this was to be her first time, then I want it to be perfect.

"It doesn't hurt." She must be reading my mind. "It's just… different."

I shudder as I press my face to her throat, begging myself to be patient. Ripples of tension clamp down around me—her body clenching around the invasion of my cock as if it's slowly surrendering to this new sensation. I run my hands over her skin to distract her, my mouth sliding over hers. Luring her into another gentle, devastating kiss.

Vi arches beneath me, then gasps. Our tongues tangle together, hot and slow. Everything is slow now. Clasping our palms together, I pin the back of her hands to the heather and then rock against her.

It feels like a wave of pressure crawls up my spine, gripping the back of my neck.

"Better?" I need to know.

She sinks her teeth into her lower lip and nods.

"Do you like this?" I thrust slowly. In and out, grinding my teeth together as she gasps and clenches.

"*Yes.*"

I kiss her throat, her chin, her mouth. I take her so slowly she's practically begging by the time I can feel tension coiling through her.

"*Harder.*" She digs her nails into my shoulders, her thighs clamping around my hips.

"Like this?" I thrust hard and she gasps again.

Teeth sink into the sensitive area where my shoulder meets my neck. A hiss escapes me. *Fuck.* I slam into her, and every inch of her flexes in supple welcome. Shoving a hand under her ass, I shift her into position until every thrust I make is grinding over that sweet little spot between her thighs.

A soft moan echoes in my ear. For all that she's new to this, she catches on quick. Hooking my arm under her knee, I haul her thigh up until I can get deeper. Sweat slicks my spine. Every breath comes as a harsh pant. But she's there…. Mouth parting in a gasp as she comes with another scream.

Finally. Permission to let myself fall over the edge with her. I chase her into pleasure, rutting into her hard.

It's her name on my lips as I come.

Vi.

Violet.

My Vi.

Her face in my head, in my heart, as I collapse against her, both of us gasping and breathless. A trembling hand runs up my spine, curling into the flesh at the base of my skull.

"Oh, my gods," she whispers. "That was…."

"Written in the stars," I tell her with a rough laugh.

Our eyes meet.

I kiss her. Hard.

This is the start of forever.

She just doesn't know it yet.

But first, I need to make amends for how I took her tonight. And she will have my apology from my hands and tongue, until she can barely take any more.

∾

MORNING LIGHT CREEPS OVER THE CLEARING, GILDING THE pair of us. Vi's shoulders rise and fall as she sleeps in my arms. There's something about the innocent way her lashes lie closed over her eyes that makes me want to hold her here forever, where I can protect her.

My fingers trail down her flank.

Her lashes flutter, her hip shifting in response to the stroke of my fingers. Not quite asleep, not quite fully awake.

But completely aware of my touch.

"You were a virgin." I kiss her shoulder, stealing a shiver from her. None of this makes sense. Lammastide is often a night for stolen pleasure, and events such as this occur regularly, but I never expected her to be a maid.

I like it though.

I like it too much.

She has never known another and now she never will. The Darkness within me purrs and stretches with content- ment. For once we're in perfect agreement.

Vi is mine—*ours*—and nothing is going to tear her from my arms.

"Mmm." Her lashes flutter open.

"I should have spanked your ass for not warning me."

Dark eyes the color of midnight come into focus as she turns her head to look at me. There's a moment where she realizes where she is and who she's with, and then her eyes go very wide and she stills.

"Good morning." I can feel her heart hammering in her chest and I can't help kissing her shoulder so she knows there's nothing to fear. "You have blue eyes. I didn't know you had blue eyes."

They'd been midnight-dark in the vision Maia gave to me, and over the years I guess I'd let memory soften them to the darkest of browns.

The tension slides out of her. Both our masks are long gone. It added a certain kind of spice to the encounter, but I want to know who she is.

"You have green eyes," she whispers, staring deep into my soul.

I don't know why, but instinct tells me she's the watchful sort. The way she looks at me tells me she sees everything. A not entirely comfortable situation, but somehow…. Nobody has ever seen the whole of me.

And I want them to, I realize.

I want her to.

Vi turns her head. "Where's my dress?"

Oh no. I've only just found you. I curl up as she pushes herself upright, tangling my arms around her. "There's no hurry."

She glances toward the sky. Dawn. I can almost read her thoughts and so I sweep her hair over one shoulder and brush a kiss against the nape of her neck.

"Stay with me," I breathe as she shudders.

"I *can't.*"

"Yes, you can." Slowly, I drag her back down to the heather. *Forever,* if need be.

Forever, whispers the Darkness and my gut goes tight with tension because I hadn't realized I'd let it slip through the cracks in my wards. *We can fuck her forever.*

I shake it away and cage it deep. Maybe it's the woman in my arms who allows me to do so this easily. It never settles without a fight, but she's here. She's mine. She's—

"Vi," I whisper, tasting her name. "Violet. You never did ask my name."

She arches back into me. "I think it's wisest if I don't know."

I freeze as things become abundantly clear.

She gave me her virginity, she was two seconds away from stealing into her dress and fleeing, and now she still doesn't want my name.

I bite her shoulder. Hard. And she squeals.

"I'm starting to feel a little used, *Violet*."

"I wouldn't have thought that would be a problem." There's a little hint of temper there. "You were the one who hunted *me* down. Is this not what you wanted?"

It's not what I wanted at all. Caught in my own fucking net. I wanted her so badly I couldn't keep my hands off her, but all she wants is *this*.

So be it. There's more than one way to catch the demi-fey.

"Fine. No names then. Just my cock."

I slide my fingers up her thigh, back and forth. Teasing. Tempting. Her breath catches.

"Open your legs," I whisper.

She's slick and wet as I find her. A breath rushes from her chest as I trace the heart of her pleasure.

"Gods, what do you do to me?" she gasps.

"Have you never touched yourself?"

Stillness. The answer is there as she shudders. *Yes*. "It's different," she whispers. "It's different with you. More... intense."

I drive a pair of fingers into her and she arches back into my embrace.

"Touch me," I demand.

Her groping hand slides between us. *Fuck.* I can't help flexing into her grip, burying my face in her nape. I could spend like this.

She nudges back into me, her intentions clear. I want to take up her silent invitation and thrust myself inside her, but I still owe her for that no names business.

Last night, she made swift work of all my intentions. I'm not going to let her do it to me again.

"Do you know what I want?" I nudge her onto her hands and knees, driving my thigh between hers as I curl my fist in her hair.

"What?" she gasps, rocking back against me.

I draw her up onto her knees and nuzzle against her neck, every inch of us plastered together. "I want you to scream for mercy, *Violet*. I want you to beg for my cock." I kiss her throat, and curl my other hand over her breast as she sinks back into me, my cock sliding through her wetness. "But most of all, I want you to scream *my name*."

"So needy," she gasps. "Is this what you demand from all the girls?"

I swat her backside. "There are no other girls."

Violet laughs, shooting me a sultry look over her shoulder. "Not anymore, anyway. I've ruined you for all others."

"You did more than that." I drive into her with a single thrust, and her inner muscles clench around me as she moans. Spearing my fingers between her thighs I work her hard. "You ruined me, Violet. I took one look into those eyes of yours and swore you'd be mine."

"Vi," she moans. "Call me Vi."

I don't know why, but I suddenly have the suspicion she hasn't been entirely truthful with me. "Were you lying to me?" I pinch her nipple. "Your name isn't Violet, is it?"

"All this talk," she gasps, "of names. What is in a name?"

"It's all the better to claim you with," I snarl, as I drive her forward onto her forearms.

She knows nothing of pleasure. She's only instinct in this moment, letting me put her where I want her. I tilt her hips until I'm riding over that spot deep within, the one I know gives so much pleasure.

And there it is.

Her breath catches. A spasm works its way through her. She gasps. "What are you—?"

"If you won't say my name, then you may call me 'my prince.'" I grind over her again, feeling heat flash through my balls. She's so fucking tight she's going to kill me.

"My handsome fairy tale prince?" There's another laugh. "That feels *so* good. I thought you intended to punish me."

Oh, she's got a defiant streak. I smile. I like it. "Maybe I will. One day. But you're too innocent to know what you're asking for."

She tenses again and I know it's the "one day". "What I'm asking for?"

I reach between her thighs and pinch her clit. Vi reacts like I've set off a bomb, her shocked body clenching around mine.

"Oh gods," she moans, resting her forehead down on her hands and arching back into me like she's begging for more. A hint of a tattoo peeks out from beneath her curtain of hair.

"Just 'my prince.'" I tease, and then I'm pushing her over the edge, pinching her again, alternating it with gentle flicks of my fingers, then back to pain again. Until she's gasping, begging me for obliteration.

"As you wish," I press down hard and fuck my way into her in long, slow strokes that make my own teeth grind together. The clench of her body is surreal. I planned on prolonging this, but there's no help for me, no use other than to come with her—

Throwing my head back, I bite my lip and spill my seed within her.

Vi shudders, her body trembling with aftershock. Little lightning jolts go through her with every brush of my hands on her hips, her thighs. I can barely hold my weight off her anymore, and as my cock slips from her warm body, we tumble into the grass together, breathing hard.

"You're beautiful when you beg me," I whisper, drawing her back into my arms. Her eyes are glazed, hair tangled across her lips. "So fucking beautiful."

Vi sinks her hand through my hair and pulls my face down to kiss her.

"You're the beautiful one," she admits, her voice rough and low as we break free of each other.

"Mmm." I brush the slickness of my seed across her thigh. "You know how to be careful?" It honestly didn't occur to me to ask last night. I took one look at her and lost all hint of common sense.

"Careful?"

I draw back to look at her. "You have a sachet of bitter nettle tea to drink?"

Though children are rare for the fae, accidents very rarely occur. Most of the females attending the rites bring little sachets with them.

Vi sits up sharply. "Oh. Yes. Yes, I can get my hands on some."

So she wasn't planning this…. Not beyond yesterday, anyway. I don't know why I like the thought of that.

Or maybe I do.

I didn't want to be just a body she chose to lose her virginity to.

"Mmm." I kiss her arm, her shoulder, her—

"Vi!" someone calls.

Her head shoots up, attention locking on the voice like a deer scenting the hounds. Shifting onto one hand, I rest my chin on her shoulder. "Who is—?"

"Vi!" Another low hiss of the word. "Where in the Underworld are you? Mother's looking for you."

Vi?

I try to reach for her but she's gone, vanishing from my arms as if she'd never been there. Whipping to her feet, she snatches at her dress and then her shoes, clearly trying to find her underwear.

"You weren't wearing any," I remind her, lying back on the grass and rubbing the heels of both hands over my face. "You don't have to go." I shoot her a lazy smile. "Your mother won't mind if you're a little late, I'm sure."

Vi shimmies into the gown, draping its loose straps over her shoulders. She shoots me a look. "You don't know her." The words are dry, and then she lifts her voice. "I'm here, Andi. Just… give me a moment."

A shadow pauses outside the thicket. "Vi?" the woman hisses. "What—? Are you—?"

"Not alone," I call out, which earns a certain scalded silence.

Vi crouches before me.

"Thank you, my handsome prince." There's an edge of wistfulness to her. "Thank you for giving me a night to remember."

Light's starting to creep through the thicket. Her gaze drops to the shadows of Darkness obliterating my chest.

"Here," she murmurs, gesturing to the back of her neck. "There's a tiny button there. Can you—?"

I brush her hair aside, finding the little pearl button among the dripping lace. It's ridiculously small, and my fingers too clumsy, but I manage it, even as the woman outside our little nest paces. There's something dark down her spine. I try to brush her hair aside to see what it is, but she slaps my fingers impatiently. "Button."

"As my lady wishes." Unable to help myself, I press a kiss to her neck. "Will I see you tonight?"

She hesitates.

"I want to see you again." Another glancing kiss. I've only just found her. I'm not letting her go now.

"I shouldn't." She glances back over her shoulder, biting that lip. "I shouldn't have given you even this. My mother…."

"Fuck your mother." I capture her chin and with it, her mouth. She tastes like sweet hesitance, but the second my tongue darts against hers, she moans and kisses me back.

"You don't understand." Vi trembles as she presses her forehead to mine. "My mother will kill you if she hears of this." Fingertips brush against my cheeks. "I just wanted…. Once. I just wanted a single night to pretend I was free to make my own choices."

Don't we all?

But there's something in the way she says it that makes me draw back and consider her heart-shaped face.

She doesn't want me to know her name.

She's scared of her mother.

There's no reason to connect the dots, but a lead weight starts to settle in my chest. Premonition, perhaps.

Then she's gone.

She peers out through the brambles, dawn's soft light pouring over her as she winds her hair into a knot and pins it atop her head. Without the cascade of her hair, her back is revealed. The dress cuts wide and dips low, revealing all of that smooth, olive skin. Skin I never truly noticed last night, when she danced in my arms. Her hair was always covering it. Gold flashes on her back. Gold and black and red…. It's a tattoo that runs down her spine, one I never noticed in the light of the stars.

One by one my eye picks out roses, and then the gold begins to make sense…. Thorns. Thorns and roses, and a gilded crown.

Everything within me goes cold.

My mother.

She's got the royal fucking crest of Asturia on her back.

"Vi." Relief floods the stranger's voice, and there's a whispered half-exchange between them that ends with,

"What were you thinking? Staying out so late? She's already asking for you!"

Vi.

Not Violet.

There are two daughters. Andraste, the Crown Princess, and…. "Iskvien."

It captures her attention. Dark eyes meet mine as I slowly push to my feet, and she looks a little confused, as if to wonder how I know her name. "Goodbye, my prince."

There's no guile in her expression.

No hint she even suspects.

She doesn't know.

And then she's gone, leaving me with the reeling sensation that fate just kicked me in the teeth.

There's only a single starburst mask, lying forlornly in the grass.

"YOU RUINED *EVERYTHING*," THALIA ACCUSES, THE SECOND I'm back within my tents. "Princess Lucere was there to meet you, and you barely even looked at her, before you ran off with another woman." She rakes her hands through her hair. "I can fix this," she says, half to herself. "I can—"

"No." There's no point in playing alliances now. "There will not be a marriage between Evernight and Ravenal."

Thalia pales. "*What*?"

I can barely breathe as I turn away from her, rubbing at my knuckles. Eris remains a silent shadow at my back. She *knows*. The queensmoot may be the only time when murder and treachery is forbidden, but I still don't go anywhere without at least her or Baylor at my back, and it seems Eris drew the short straw last night.

She'd have given me enough distance to have some semblance of privacy, but when I finally exited my heather-scented bower, she'd arched an eyebrow at me.

"Out." I tilt my head toward the door. I need to bathe and dress. I need a fucking moment alone to still the thoughts circling my head like sharks.

She's Asturian.

It's a fist within my chest. A knot of discordant emotion.

She's fucking Asturian. My promise, my hopes, my dreams…. They're all turning into a nightmare.

Because Adaia will never allow me to touch one of her precious daughters.

The daemon within me laughs. *Did you think it would be that easy?*

"Out?" Thalia repeats, as if she's never heard the word before. She sets her hands on her hips. "Did you just tell me to get out of your tents?"

I wasn't thinking. "Please," I add. "I need to bathe."

Oh, it's too late for that. Her eyes narrow. "What's wrong? Why do you look like you were just punched in the sternum. Eris?"

She looks to Eris, who is pouring a glass of wine.

For breakfast.

"What is going on here?" Thalia demands.

"Thanks," I mutter, as Eris turns with the wine.

She merely arches her brow at me. "Who said it was for you?"

And then she drains it.

I pour my own.

"It was the woman, wasn't it?" Thalia's apparently scented blood, and she's smart enough to put it all together. "The way you went after her—"

"It's *her*," I tell her.

There's a moment where she doesn't understand, and then the color bleeds from her cheeks. "*Her*? The one you saw all those years ago?"

I nod.

She clasps her hands over her mouth. "Mother of Night." Thoughts race through her eyes. "Clearly, things went well between you…. And you've finally found her. I don't understand what the problem is."

"The problem is," Eris says to Thalia, "that she's fucking Asturian. Adaia's youngest daughter by the look of her. Lysander was supposed to watch Thiago's back last night and I traded in with him sometime after three so he could get some sleep." She jacks her thumb toward me. "I didn't realize who our prince was cuddling up with until this morning, when it was too late. Or I would have put a halt to it."

"Asturian?" Thalia whispers in horror.

"Don't look at me like that," I snap. "I didn't know who she was either, until I saw the tattoo down her back."

"You didn't think to ask?" she demands.

"She *lied*. She said her name was Vi. For Violet." It's a troubling thought, because surely Vi didn't know who I was. She would never have lain with me if she did.

But why lie about it?

Is it because her mother wouldn't approve?

She was a virgin. She couldn't hide that.

She also couldn't hide the fact she'd been fairly determined to get rid of her innocence, because I was content to wait.

This is a nightmare.

If Adaia catches wind of this, she'll have me murdered.

"Maybe you can use this," Eris points out. "You were talking about kidnapping the younger princess, after all."

I shoot her a glare. That was before I realized she's the woman I've been searching for all my life.

"Or not," Thalia says swiftly.

I tug the mask from my pocket, rubbing my fingers over the sequins. "Can you please—the both of you—just give me a moment alone?"

Eris slams the goblet down, bows her head and then vanishes.

Thalia, however, pauses before me, her eyes on the mask. "This doesn't mean it's the end of everything," she whispers. "I know how much she means to you."

"She means nothing." My voice is raw. "Because she's a stranger."

Thalia kisses me cheek. "You've spent five hundred years wishing her to life. Don't give up now just because we've faced a brief setback."

"We?" I can barely say the words. "I thought you were all for the alliance with Ravenal?"

Thalia sighs. "Fuck Ravenal. It was a good plan. But this is forever, Thi." She steps away from me a little wistfully. "You don't throw the god's gifts in their face."

"Even if they're your enemy's daughter?"

She bites her lip. "Maybe it's time for peace? Maybe this is how we finally win it?"

I tap the mask against my lips, breathing in the scent of Vi. She's all night-blooming Sorrow flowers and sweetness; moonlight and roses. "Maybe."

The problem is, I know Adaia far too well to ever believe she'll agree to peace.

6

ISKVIEN

E xhilaration buzzes over my skin as I head for my mother's tent, my wet hair knotted at the base of my skull. I washed and dressed before the summons came, but the fact remains that something irrefutable changed within me last night.

Before I kissed a stranger, I was Iskvien, a caged princess facing a marriage she despises.

Now there's a throbbing beat of defiance in my chest. *No, no, no*, it says, in time with my heartbeat. I know the cost of defiance. To deny this contract with Etan will earn me untold punishment, but the wildness within me can't be tamed.

I don't know what to do.

Last night was just a dream, a mirage, but it feels like a jolt of magic injected straight into my veins. It was more than I ever expected it to be, and now that I've known the touch of another man, I can't help thinking that I could never submit to Etan.

I can still feel my stranger's hands on my skin. I can

taste his mouth. The imprint of his cock between my thighs.

I am worth more than this. I will not have my future stolen, simply because my mother will score some political points.

Now I just have to tell her.

Sounds echo from within Mother's tent as I approach.

Something strikes flesh with a whistling grace, and a harsh grunt fills the air.

I know that sound. Mother's got her whip in hand. I've felt the bite of it once or twice, but the worst part is when she coils it around her hand, length by length, her eyes locking upon you as she advances.

My body refuses to move another inch and a cold sweat breaks out down my spine. She can't know what happened last night. We managed to lose the ever-present guard who follows me at all times. But what if... she found out?

What if my handsome stranger knew who I was?

What if he said something to someone and they told Mother?

It's ridiculous. The amount of coincidences to achieve such a thing are too great.

But my feet itch to turn around and vanish back into the tent city.

So much for defiance. One flick of the whip and you're already looking for ways to submerge into the Old Iskvien.

I force a slow breath through my lungs. It's chilling how easy it would be to let defiance smolder to ashes. *Be brave, be brave, be brave.*

Besides, it's too late. The guards are looking at me and

87

one of them draws the canvas flap back, ushering me inside.

If I make her wait, she'll only have me dragged before her.

I duck into the gloom of the tent.

There's a stranger on his knees, his brown hair sweat-drenched and bloody, and his shirt clinging to him in strips. Raw flesh encircles his wrists—a sure sign of weeks worth of manacles, if not months.

"Fuck you," the stranger says, tilting his head back. He pushes off his knuckles and knees and—

"Ah ah ah, Finn," Edain says, setting one hand on the stranger's shoulder and forcing him back to the floor. His eyes never leave my mother's back, and the way he's fingering the knife in his other hand makes me wonder just who he intends to use it upon. "My queen said you were to remain on your knees."

The stranger laughs under his breath. "Is that what you do for her, Pet? Does she make you get on your knees too? Do you grovel before her and—"

Edain moves so fast it's a flashing blow. The stranger's head whips to the side, where it remains for a moment as if he's gathering his breath. "You shouldn't speak of my queen like that," Edain says, but there's a flare of rage within his eyes.

It's not loyalty.

It's not for the insult to the queen.

Does Edain despise his role as much as I do?

"Iskvien." Mother's chest heaves as she coils the whip. "Where have you been?"

Picking grass out of my hair. I take smooth, cautious

steps closer, trying to read the room. "Bathing. As one does when one wakes."

Andraste sits stiffly in a chair beside Mother's throne, her gaze drilling right through me as if she alone can see exactly what happened. Tendrils of Mother's hair wisp around her braids, as if she's been wielding the whip hard. And Edain cuts me an insolent look, as if he doesn't like me seeing him in this state.

But it's the stranger my eyes are drawn to.

There's a strange tattoo between his brows. It almost looks like the golden outline of a flame, but it's so faint it's difficult to make out against his golden skin. He's gorgeous. All of the fae are, but there's something about the chiseled slant of his cheekbones, that sulky mouth and the alpine blue of his eyes that makes my breath catch. It must be killing Mother to keep her hands off him. I swear I've seen a tattoo like that somewhere before, but I've never seen his face. Of that I'm sure of.

"What's going on?"

Mother casts the whip aside and wipes her hands on a rag. "Nothing that need concern you. What took you so long to answer my summons?"

"Maybe she's avoiding you," Finn says with a rough laugh. "Can't imagine why…."

The presence of the stranger throws me off-balance. I expected her fury, but I also expected to be the center of its attention, and from the look she gives the wounded warrior, I'm not.

"If he speaks again, cut out his tongue," Mother says.

Edain shifts on his feet and he and the stranger share an intimate look.

"I was celebrating Lammastide," I reply, trying to swallow down the guilt in my throat. I barely had time to wash the scent of my handsome lover from my skin. "Is that not why we're here? I woke in a glade somewhere near the forest and it took time to return."

"Why we're *here*? The queen of Ravenal is waiting for us in her tent," she snaps. "Her nephew is there. Etan. You may remember him. You were supposed to dance with him last night, but you vanished in the middle of the unmasking—"

Heat and rage smolder in my gut like an ember. Here it is. Here's my moment. Deep breath. *Be brave.* "Apparently I'm supposed to do many things, Mother, but I will point out that nobody ever asked *me* if I wanted to do them."

Stillness coils through her. "You've heard."

"I've heard *something*," I point out. "Etan managed to tell me the most ridiculous lie. I couldn't quite believe it, because I *know* you would never stoop so low as to sell me to that pathetic worm—"

"Careful, Iskvien," she warns as she turns toward her wine. "My mood is much improved, but I won't tolerate such disrespect. And Etan is merely a stepping stone to a greater game. He's not lying. You will marry him. You will do Asturia proud."

"He's a wretched—"

"He's the nephew of Queen Maren," she counters. "And you are *my* daughter. Are you saying that you are too weak to handle him? Are you saying that my own flesh and blood cannot manipulate a witless reprobate like Etan? You disappoint me. I offer you a means to step into the Askan court and build a power base. I *gave* you an introduction. Why did you think I sent you to serve Maren?"

Because I still can't access my magic, and you were so furious with me you could barely look me in the eye. "What kind of power base can I build? Etan's only influence lies with the younger fae at court. He spends half his days drinking, the other half chasing sprites around the palace. He's not Maren's heir. He's not even among the top ten on the list to *be* heir—"

"That can change," she warns.

I reel back. "Oh, wonderful. Now I'm supposed to add assassination to my repertoire, am I?"

"Not you." She doesn't quite look at Edain. "Too many mysterious deaths in a short time would provide… uncomfortable scrutiny. But one or two might be overlooked. The Askan court is ambitious, and with Maren unable to give the court a true heir, the rest of them will climb all over each other like mountain goats. No, your task is to remain unnoticed. Bide your time, like a spider.

"I give you a gift, Iskvien. The boy is an idiot. Gullible, easily controlled. He sees only flesh to own, and a will to conquer. Let him think that. Move behind the scenes. Build your base. Birth a child or two. You can never rule the Askan court yourself, but you could place a puppet on the throne. Whether that is your husband or your daughter is your choice." Her voice roughens. "But you *will* do this for me."

It feels like a whirlpool, sucking me toward some hideous fate.

To defy her means punishment. She's never baulked at any cruelties.

Memory chokes me....

"Wield the flame, Iskvien."

My gut knots up tight as she brings the candle closer. I can't stop a hint of dread from breaking over my skin in chills. My magic's been slow to come in, and my mother thinks forcing me into these training sessions will help me, but if anything, my ability to weave fire is getting worse.

"Touch the flame," she says.

"I can't," I cry, and it's a little girl's voice.

"You will." There's no mercy in her voice. "Whether you touch it with your magic, or with your skin is the choice you must make. I will not have a weak daughter."

I break free of that moment, sweat dripping down my spine.

There's no sign of a burn on my skin anymore—my fae blood is strong enough to heal almost anything she can do to me—but I can feel it there, like a scar that sunk into my bones.

The question is: How far do I dare defy her?

What could be worse? My mother's certain punishment, or marriage with Etan? It's only trading one monster for another.

And yet....

There's the memory of a kiss on my lips.

There's a flame of defiance in my heart burning faster and faster....

"I won't marry him," I whisper.

"Pardon?" My mother spins toward me, as if she can't quite believe her ears.

I force myself to meet her gaze. "I will *not* marry Etan."

"Do you defy me, Iskvien?"

I don't want this to happen here, with Edain watching, but there's no help for it.

"He's a monster," I blurt. "He's cruel and—"

"I don't care." Movement flashes toward me and her fingers dig into my jaw. "I don't care if Etan fucks you into the stone of the court. I don't care if he locks you away in a tower. He will not harm you. He will not dare. But I set no limits on his being kind to you. If you were strong, if you had your magic, then you could make him sweat. Your weakness is your own fault. Your inability to force him to dance to your tune is your own fault. You want to be weak? Then you will suffer your own consequences." She shakes her head. "I can give you everything, Iskvien, but you have failed me again and again and again. I must find some means to turn your birth to my advantage. You *will not fail me* this final time."

"Mother," Andraste starts.

Mother stabs a finger toward my sister, though she doesn't tear her gaze away from me. "Not another word."

I tear my chin free of her grasp. To speak now is dangerous, but I'm so fucking tired of biting my tongue. "If I am weak it is because you have made me so. I remember, Mother. I *remember* what you did to me."

The blow snaps my head to the side, and I stagger back, fists coming up protectively to defend myself against the next one—

It never comes.

Instead, Edain is there, one hand manacled around my mother's wrist. "My queen."

"*What*?" she demands, violence seething through her green eyes. "You *dare* lay hands on me?"

"I dare urge caution." He brings her hand to his lips. "The tent walls are thin and soldiers gossip. We don't know how many of our people are loyal, and how many of them work for other queens. Maren's no fool. She *cannot* hear of this. She cannot afford to see any bruises left on Iskvien's skin."

"Iskvien will heal."

"Not before your meeting."

Mother rips her wrist from his grasp and turns on her heels to pace, her skirts slithering after her. But there's a thoughtful gleam in her eyes. "You're right. You're always right, my love."

I don't know if he just saved me from a true beating.

He despises me and the feeling is mutual.

But if he hadn't interrupted just then….

A murderous look comes into her eyes and her smile becomes a sharp edge.

Oh no. I recognize that look.

"I cannot leave a mark on my dearest Iskvien's skin," she whispers, stalking toward me. "I can't harm a hair on her head. You want to play these games, my *dearest child*? Then let us play them."

Mother draws the jeweled knife from her hip and turns toward the stranger on his knees. Finn tilts his face toward her defiantly, and it's not until she sets the tip of the knife to the hollow beneath his eye that I see the flicker of his pulse kick in his throat.

"No!" I lunge toward her, but a single bead of blood drips down his cheek and I freeze.

I remember this game.

I remember what she did to Nanny Redwyne, when my nurse begged for mercy for me.

"No, no, please. Don't."

The entire room is still.

Edain follows the movement of my mother's knife like a charmed snake. Gone is the insolence, the grace, the lounging pet. Instead, he's a coil of tension, prepared to move at a moment's notice.

"Adaia," he warns.

But I don't know what he's warning against.

Finn freezes, leaning back into her touch as if to escape the pressure of the knife. Maybe my urgency has finally made him realize this is no game.

"I offered the bastard of Evernight a trade," my mother whispers with a savage glee. The knife digs into the flesh beneath Finn's eye. "Maybe I'll send him a little gift to convince him. What say you, Iskvien? Go ahead. Defy me. Tell me you won't do as you're told. Tell me you won't marry Etan." She throws her head back and laughs. "Every time you defy me, I'll cut another piece off him."

Her knife starts to slide through skin and Finn screams, jerking back into her, helpless with his hands bound behind him and the iron collar shackled around his throat.

"Maybe we'll start with an eye."

"Stop!" It's a scream, a desperate pledge. "Stop! I'll sign the marriage contract." The words burst from my throat. "I'll sign it."

Mother stills. "What did you say?"

I slump to my hands and knees. I want to be sick.

"I'll sign the marriage contract." The words are dull.

Empty. There goes my defiance. But first…. I look up. "Let him go. Unharmed. Promise me you will not hurt him and I will give you what you desire."

"Oh, Iskvien." She looks almost disappointed in me. "You're so easy to manipulate. I promise."

"Promise it thrice. On your power. On your throne." Because I'm not falling for that trick.

"I promise that I will not hurt him."

"Now or ever," I counter. "You will not instruct any other hand to cause harm to him either."

She concedes with a faint little smile, and repeats herself twice more.

I've earned some reprieve by holding her to account.

She hates my empathy, but she'd despise my stupidity even more.

"Done," I whisper, as the magic of Mother's oath sweeps around her and binds us together.

Mother shoves the stranger forward and he hits the ground face first. But I can see his wild eyes, finding mine. Blood drips from the little wedge she's carved from the skin beneath his eye.

We stare at each other for a frozen moment.

I'm sorry, I want to say.

And I don't even know what for, because I'm not the one who put him in chains. I have no power here. I can't change his circumstances.

And to even breathe those words with my mother in the room will earn him more than an unkind death.

"Get up." Mother steps over him and sweeps toward me as if she didn't just threaten to cut his eye out, right in front of me. "Get up and straighten your skirts. You are my daughter and you will not appear before Maren looking like some slovenly slattern."

I can barely breathe, but somehow my body pushes itself to its feet. I move like a puppet on her strings.

There has to be some way out of this mess.

I can't just give in.

I won't.

But... how?

I'll sign the contracts, I promised. But I never said I'd marry him.

The world slows down around me as I lift my gaze to my mother.

She wants me to learn how to be manipulative?

She wants me to learn to play the game?

So be it. It's a heady, unbalancing thought. I don't even know what I can do, but now it feels like there are options out there if I can just find them.

"What am I supposed to do with him?" Edain calls, reminding us both of Finn's presence.

Mother stills, casting the stranger a hard look.

"I urge a cautious response," Edain tells her. "Finn can still be useful to us. Perhaps Evernight won't pay your price for him, but the prince is known to be loyal to his men. If he wants his little pet back, then he'll have to agree to some sort of arrangement."

"Fuck you." This Finn spits a bloodied gobbet of spittle at Edain and bares blood-stained teeth in a smile.

Edain tears a silk square from his pocket and wipes the blood off his hand and shirt. "Careful now. We're bartering with your life, and I seem to be the only one who gives a damn if you live or die."

"Kill me then. I'll die for my prince here and now if it will spare him your trap."

The loyalty in this Finn's eyes steals my breath, because nobody in my mother's court would ever offer their life for her like that.

"Throw him back in his cage," Mother finally says, before her fingers dig into my wrist. "I care not. If Evernight can be brought to heel, then I will have him grovel at my feet. Right now...." She wrenches me cruelly toward the door flap of the tent. "My daughter and I go to greet the queen of Ravenal and pay her respects." Her fingers leave cruel marks on my arm. "And she *will* be signing a marriage contract today."

7

ISKVIEN

If Mother was surprised by my smile when I greeted Maren, and the easy grace with which I signed my name to a marriage contract between Aska and Asturia, there's no sign of it on her face as she leads us into the heart of the Hallow.

I keep waiting for the lash to fall but it occurs to me that the reason she doesn't suspect something devious in my heart is because I've never dared openly defy her before.

She thinks me cowed.

We climb toward the Hallow.

It's a nexus point where leylines meet, and we used it to arrive here yesterday morning. The power of the Hallow can be used as a portal, except one is bound by the leylines. You can only travel to another nexus point, another Hallow.

It's also the place where the Seelie Alliance meets whilst at the queensmoot, and there is to be a gathering of the heads of the alliance.

The gently sloping hill is capped with ruins, with the Hallow right in the center. It's a sacred place and to spill blood here is forbidden. Each queen is allowed to bring five guards only, and the space around the Hallow has been cleared for two hundred yards around it so that any threat can be seen coming.

The enormous standing stones of the Hallow cast ominous shadows as we walk between them.

Some still bear lintels; enormous wedges of stone somehow hauled on top of a pair of sentinel stones. Other lintel stones lie cracked and shattered at their feet. Some of the scholars at the Akvaran University in Aska have tried to study this Hallow, and believe they've found the quarry where the stone came from—nearly a hundred miles away from this place.

Nobody has been able to fathom how the otherkin who once ruled this world managed to get those stones into place. Their tools were primitive, their magics bound to the Hallows and their gods. And yet the floor of this partic- ular Hallow is polished slate so smooth it almost seems like an obsidian mirror. Bronze glyphs are etched into the stone, and research has proven that on certain nights of the year, moonlight will spill through little holes in the sentinel stones to create a perfect circle of moonlight on each glyph.

It wasn't just a portal to the otherkin.

It wasn't just a place of worship and sacrifice.

It was also a calendar of all the celestial events.

Five golden thrones have been brought into the Hallow.

We're the last to arrive.

"Greetings, Adaia," calls Queen Maren, her smooth dark hair tumbling in a silken fall over her shoulders. A black crown circles her head, the points akin to a spear. She's rumored to be the most beautiful woman in the world, and if she's not, then she's very close to the top of the list.

Lucidia of Ravenal slouches in her chair, looking irritable. She clutches a shawl around her shoulders as if she feels the cold, and maybe she does, because age is starting to settle over her face and hair like a mantle. The fae live for enviously long centuries, but Lucidia has taken that first step toward the grave.

It doesn't make her any less dangerous.

She squints in our direction. "You're late."

"My apologies." My mother leads us toward the throne in front of the Asturian standard. "I had a little… issue to deal with within my camp."

"One can believe that," says a deep, masculine voice that picks the pronunciation of every word out carefully.

My entire body clenches as if he murmured those words directly into my ear.

That voice.

My head whips toward the Prince of Evernight's throne and the breath drives from my lungs as if a fist slammed into my sternum. He looks like a prince from a fairy tale, but I know better; I've had those hands on my skin in every way possible. This man is no hero. He's the villain, and temptation is his crime.

The prince stares at me expressionlessly. If not for the intense gleam in his green eyes, I'd almost think us strangers. But it's there. The heat. The memory. The challenge. That soft mouth is pressed into a thin line, his cheekbones sharp enough to cut butter. I can feel that mouth moving over my skin, his tongue tracing lazy circles around my navel as he dips his head lower.

Of them all, he alone doesn't bother to wear a crown.

He doesn't need to.

There's no denying this male has power. There's no denying he's dangerous. Clad in a black velvet doublet, he reclines at ease, both arms resting along the arms of his throne.

And he looks at me as if we share a secret and he's just dying to ask me more about it.

Even though I half-expected it from the second I heard him speak, shock ripples through me as I stare into my lover's eyes.

The Prince of Evernight.

I fucked my mother's dearest enemy.

Oh, my gods.

My heart skips a beat and the blood drains from my face. Shock turns my feet clumsy, and I trip over absolutely nothing, slamming into Edain. My stepbrother grabs me, leaving me tangled uncomfortably in his arms with my nose driving into his velvet-clad chest.

This is the single most embarrassing way to make my official welcome to the alliance, and I can practically feel my mother's glare searing the back of my neck as Edain sets me to rights.

"Iskvien?" Edain murmurs.

"S-sorry." I brush the velvet nap free of the indentation of my face and then realize I'm rubbing my stepbrother's chest right in front of everyone.

His eyebrows shoot up.

He freezes.

Please, please swallow me whole, I silently beg the Hallow.

A shiver runs through the slate beneath us, gravel skittering across the ground. It's enough to tear everyone's eyes from my face and I dart behind my mother's throne, not daring to look at anyone as I hide behind Andraste.

Especially the Prince of Evernight.

I scrape a trembling hand over my mouth.

What am I going to do?

I bedded the enemy.

I fucked the Prince of Evernight, and in doing so, I gave him the gift that my mother has promised Etan.

My *virginity*.

Even if he didn't know who I was, he knows now and I am drowning so deep.

Oh, I understand the rules of the game. Of court. My mother and Thiago are enemies. And he knows she wouldn't approve of what happened. He holds all the power right now. A single smirk, a handful of words, and he has my mother over a barrel. Worse, he has a knife at *my* throat.

THERE IS TORTURE, AND THEN THERE IS AN HOUR SPENT furiously staring at my toes as the alliance barters and bargains.

Evernight was curiously quiet, and I just *know* he spent the entire time watching me. I was barely even aware of

Etan, clearing his throat at Maren's side every now and then as if to try and capture my attention.

I just wanted it to be over.

And then the gods finally granted my wishes.

"What in the Underworld was that?" My mother hisses as we safely pass through the tent line that marks Asturian territory. "Were you *trying* to humiliate me?"

I've had an hour to come up with a reasonable excuse and I have nothing. "I wasn't watching where I was going and I tripped. I'm sorry."

"I intended to present you to my fellow queens officially, and you bumble in looking like some pathetic milkmaid off her family's farm." She steps into my space, pushing her face close to me. "I don't want to see you again tonight. Andraste," she snaps to my sister. "See Iskvien to her tents. She can spend the night inside it, reflecting on her foolishness. No dancing. No singing. No wine. No dinner."

As far as punishments go, it's infinitely better than I was expecting.

My sister stays by my side as my mother stalks toward her tents, Edain following like a well-trained shadow.

"Come," Andraste says.

This is the hardest part, because my sister knows me best. I might have fooled the others, but I can sense Andraste's curiosity.

She waits until we're safely inside my tent to look at me, however. "You never trip over your own feet. I've seen you with a sword in hand. Your footwork is excellent."

"My footwork *is* excellent," I admit. "It's my heart

that's the issue." I square my shoulders. "The last two days have been one shock after the other, and the second Etan smiled at me...." I shrug.

Her eyes narrow. "Etan wasn't there when we arrived."

"Really?"

"Really."

I sink onto my bed. "Maybe I conjured him then."

"Maybe you're lying through your teeth," she says, crossing her arms. "What's going on?"

I shoot her a sour look. It's not that I don't entirely trust this sudden peace she seems to be offering—because I don't—but I so desperately want to believe it's real.

"Do you remember what you suggested I do last night?"

Her eyes widen.

"He was there today. I wasn't expecting to see him again."

"The man you were with this morning? The man you kissed?"

"It was a little more to it than that."

Her eyebrows shoot up. She didn't ask. Merely chided me for not returning sooner.

"You don't have to look so surprised," I retort. "You were the one who suggested it."

"Yes, but...." She paces within my tent. "You're always so... so..."

"So what?"

"Prim," she admits, as if she's chosen the word carefully. "You've barely even kissed before."

"The last time I kissed someone," I snap, "I found out he'd been keeping a mistress for our entire relationship.

105

And there's hardly anyone I'd consider at mother's court. They're all either in her pocket, or trying to kiss her shoes." I hug my knees to my chest. "I don't want to be a prize or a sign of her favor. I just want…."

"What?"

Love. It's a foolish little dream. I choke it down where she can't see it. "I just want to meet someone I can trust. Someone who cares for me. A little. Someone who looks at me and sees me. Iskvien. Not my mother's pawn. Not a means for advancement, or a means for revenge."

Revenge. There. I've said it, and now my entire soul locks on that word I've been trying not to even think about.

Why did the Prince of Evernight focus on me?

Because he did. He took one look at me and he had to have me, and I fell into his arms like a pathetic little virgin.

It can't have been coincidence, and I think I hate that more than anything.

Did he fuck me so he could gloat about it to my mother? Or his court?

What was last night all about?

Why did he give me such control?

What does any of it mean?

"Who was he?" Andraste murmurs, sinking onto the bed beside me.

"I don't even know," I say hastily. "Just a… retainer in some other court."

Andraste gives me a long, slow look.

"Someone I shouldn't have slept with," I snap. "Congratulate me on being a fool. I earned it."

She sighs and leans back on her hands. "Do you know why I wanted you to find someone?"

Stillness creeps through my heart. We haven't confided in each other like this for years. "Why?"

Andraste stares blankly at the tent wall in front of her. "Because I wanted one of us to be happy. I want that for you, Vi." Her lashes obscure her eyes. "Because none of the rest of us are ever going to get it."

I swallow. Hard. "I'm trapped by a marriage contract I can't get out of. I'm fairly certain that's not my happily-ever-after."

"You promised Mother you would sign Maren's contract," she replies astutely. "Don't think I didn't notice the exact words you used." She pushes to her feet, looking far older than me in this moment. "I don't know how you can get out of this arrangement, but I do know you have a chance. You have time, Vi. You want to make your own choices? Then start playing the game. You don't have the luxury of being a little girl anymore. Fight her. Fight back. But don't do it overtly."

That's easy for her to say....

She's the favored one. She can do no wrong. She's so fucking perfect it makes my heart squeeze up tight and small.

"I'll think about it," I mutter.

Andraste pauses with her hand on the tent flap. "I shouldn't ask, but was it good? Was he kind to you?"

I sink my chin into my knees, heat flaring through my cheeks.

She laughs. "Good. I'm glad he was chivalrous enough

to show you what pleasure means. Now stop being a little pet. Unsheathe your claws and play that bitch right back."

Then she's gone and I notice she didn't push me on the details.

Because she doesn't want to know.

If she doesn't know, then she can't betray me.

I don't know why that little thought gives me heart. Maybe my relationship with my sister isn't entirely ruined.

"Maybe you should count your blessings," I grumble to myself, "because at least you don't have to dance with Etan tonight."

I sink back onto my narrow bed, hauling the blankets up over my face.

What am I going to do? How did this happen?

"Why did you let me do this?" I beg Maia.

There's no answer from the goddess.

There never is.

I groan and roll onto my side, and as I do, paper crinkles near my ear. Odd. I throw the blankets back, but there's nothing there. Running a hand beneath my pillow, I find a folded scrap of parchment, barely two inches wide.

Meet me, it says. *Same time. Same place. We need to talk.*

I sit up abruptly. How did it get in here? Mother's encampment is almost more formidable than a prison when she's at camp.

I've never seen that writing before, but I know who it belongs to. There's an impatient slant to the letters as if it was written in a hurry.

Or as if he wrote it several times before screwing up each individual attempt, and finally jotted down the basics.

We need to talk.

My heart skips a beat. To meet him is foolish and dangerous.

But it I don't, then what will he do? What will he say?

Will he tell my mother?

Was I right? *Is* this revenge?

Or just the opening play in a sick and twisted game?

The prince of Evernight holds a knife to my throat with this knowledge, and I need to know how to protect myself from it.

IT'S NOT DIFFICULT TO SLIP AWAY FROM THE ASTURIAN camp.

The guards are all watching without.

And I'm the invisible daughter.

Throwing a cloak over my shoulders, I draw the hood over my hair and then slip into the forest, avoiding the bonfires and revelry as much as I can.

The little bower where I lay with the Prince of Evernight stands empty. There's no one nearby, the party having moved closer to the lake. I don't know if that's an ominous sign or not.

Crickets chirp as I pace back and forth.

The moon picks out every single night-blooming Sorrow flower. They slowly unfurl, opening their faces to its soft light, little firefly lights dancing around their petals. Demi-fey by the look of it, stealing nectar until they're Sorrow-drunk.

"You came."

I spin around, one hand dropping to the hilt of the knife sheathed at my hip and the other staring into the shadows beneath the trees. My heart pounds with a mix of dread and something I can't name. "Of course, I came."

How could I not?

He can ruin me with a single sentence.

The same way he ruined me with a kiss.

"I didn't think you were going to," he says. "You would barely look at me today."

"I was trying not to give myself away. You didn't seem to have any such compunctions. Come into the light."

Thiago seems to melt out of the shadows. Black leather encases his chest and shoulders in woven strips that delineate each hard muscle. His cloak flows down his back. The entire outfit is stark and imposing, the impact of it only heightened by the fact he towers over me. There's no sign of a crown. No rings. Not a single hint that he's royal.

He doesn't need them.

He makes Etan look like some sort of dandelion seed of a lad, pampered and spoiled and soft.

Power lingers in the direct look he gives me. The predator is leashed for the moment, but there's a hint of hunger in his eyes. I saw that look last night, as if he wanted to consume me. It's there again right now, and I can't help feeling the slick of heat that traces wet fingers between my thighs.

I can feel him again, teeth sinking into my shoulder as he thrusts inside me, a roughened growl echoing in his throat—

And no, I'm not thinking of that.

I can't afford to.

Because that was last night, when he was merely a handsome stranger.

And now he's the enemy with a knife at my throat.

"We need to talk." His expression locks down hard and tight.

It's like the words set me free. I hold up the note between two fingers. "So you said."

"Last night—"

"Last night was a mistake." I curl the note into my fist as he steps closer to me. "I had *no* idea who you were." My breath catches, but I have to ask. "Did you know?"

"No." Feral heat lights up his eyes as he leans toward me. "Not until this morning when I saw that fucking mark on your back when you slipped from my arms."

He could be lying.

I swallow, trying to force my reckless heartbeat to steady.

"What are you going to do?" Somehow, my voice comes out crisp and cool. I've spent years watching my mother rule her court. I reach down deep inside myself and summon the part of her that's within me.

I am a princess of Asturia, and if you expect me to beg for mercy, then you shall be left wanting.

His eyes narrow as if he's sorting through my words. "Do?"

"You hold the winning cards in your hand," I say coldly. "But I warn you that my mother won't take kindly to the knowledge of what happened between us."

"I didn't think she would."

"She won't cede Mistmark to you. Not for me."

"That's what you think I'm here for?" Anger roughens

111

his voice and he takes a step toward me. "You think this has anything to do with your mother?"

"You came for me." I can see it all over again. "The second you saw my face across the clearing you came for me as if you knew me. Tell me this isn't some sort of game. Tell me that you didn't think to use me against my mother."

"I. Had. *No*. Idea." His eyes look almost black in the night. "And if I was going to play a game with your mother, then I certainly wouldn't play this one." His expression retreats into itself. "It's only bound to cause more pain than pleasure."

I can't help noticing he doesn't say *no*.

Lies are difficult for the fae. It creates a world where we step carefully around our words.

"I don't believe you. I'm not *that* beautiful." It's something I've been hearing all my life. Smaller than my mother and sister. Dark of hair and eyes, where they're tall, slim and golden. "I've hardly got the kind of face that would set kings to war over me. But you took one look at me, and you wanted me. Tell me the truth."

"It *is* the truth." For the first time he looks discomforted. "You *are* beautiful. You took my breath the first moment I saw you. I could barely speak for want of you." He shakes his head a little savagely. "You have no idea the kind of warmth your smile lights within me."

My heart knots up very tight and small at the words.

I thought I'd grown used to being unloved. I'd hardened the callus around my heart, and told myself I didn't care for such emotions. Kindness is a weakness. Friendship a dream. And love is a peculiar kind of torture.

But it's like Thiago somehow senses the chink in my shields, because I feel those words in my heart like rain after a long endless run of drought.

"I looked at you and I was helpless to stay away, helpless to resist." He rakes his hand through his hair a little savagely. "You want the truth, Princess? Then here it is. Wanting you is the worst thing that could ever happen to me. Your mother captured a very dear friend of mine. My intention when I arrived at the queensmoot was to get my friend back at any cost. I even jokingly suggested to my friends that kidnapping you and using you as a bargaining chip might be an option."

I step away from him sharply.

Thiago holds his hands up in surrender. "I would never do that. It was a joke. A stupid fucking joke the gods must have been listening to. Meeting you—what happened between us last night—is like taking a sword to my plans and obliterating them. If your mother realizes I laid one hand on your head, she'll slit Finn's throat and deliver his head to me. I can't afford that. I shouldn't be here, talking to you right now. I shouldn't have stared at you this afternoon. I should pretend we'd never met and walk away and forget you."

I hadn't even thought about Finn. "Then why don't you?"

"Because of this."

He steps into me, one hand sliding behind my nape as he hauls me toward him.

Thiago's mouth crashes down upon mine and I freeze as he lays siege to my mouth.

The kiss takes me by surprise.

It's hot, possessive, controlling. Every inch of it is a statement: *You're mine*.

There's nothing sweet about this kiss. Nothing gentle. My fists curl in his shirt—partly to push him away, I think —but as the taste of him overwhelms me, I realize that wasn't what I was planning at all.

He draws back, as if sensing my hesitance. But it's too late. It was too late the second he touched me.

I kiss him back. Hard.

It's like I give him permission. Sliding a hand down my spine, he sinks those firm fingers into my ass and hauls me against him. Everything is heat. He could set me alight with a single kiss and when his tongue strokes against mine, my entire body wilts into his embrace. *This*. I want this. A shiver runs through me as if the lash of his tongue echoes within. I can practically feel it between my thighs and my mind rewards me of a flashback of last night, when he laid waste to the slit between my thighs.

The enemy.

I'm kissing the enemy.

What are you doing? whispers the part of me that I really should listen to. Common sense, perhaps.

But common sense dictates I shove him away from him, demand that he won't tell a soul about this, and then return to my tent where I will never see him again. Common sense would have me bound at the wrist to Etan, forced into his bed and his life and shackled by every whim he ever has. Common sense is what has made me hold my tongue all these years, when my mother stared me down.

Common sense needs to die a convenient death.

There's no reason to this. Nothing beyond need. And maybe there's a little part of me that likes that it's him I'm kissing. This is freedom. My mother would kill me if she knew I was here, and there's a vindictive sort of pleasure in knowing that.

It's Thiago who breaks the kiss first, resting his forehead against mine and breathing hard. "You ruin me," he rasps. "All my good intentions…. Gone."

"Likewise." Pleasure hammers through my veins. I splay my hand over his chest, digging my fingertips into the hard muscle there. I barely had a chance to explore last night.

Thiago's eyes open and he stares down at me, a dangerous smile curling over his mouth. "This is so wrong."

"I know." The whisper is torn from my lips.

"I don't want to stop. I don't want to end this." His thumb brushes over my breast, scraping against my nipple. "But I won't have a repeat of last night."

"What was wrong with last night?"

His mouth twists. "The second I touched you, I lost control. I was inside you before I could barely have a chance to explore." He lifts my wrist to his mouth, pressing a kiss to the inside of my pulse. "And trust me, Princess. I want to explore."

A shiver runs all the way through me as his tongue traces over those delicate veins.

"I—"

He suddenly freezes.

"What? What's wrong?"

He captures my hand, pushing the sleeve of my gown

115

higher until he can see the ring of bruises around my wrist. His touch is far more careful than it ought to be. Almost as if he can't bear to see those marks that mar my olive skin.

I wrench my hand back to my chest. "Don't."

Our eyes meet, and there's something dark and dangerous stirring within him, something intense that traps me in its spell, until the world drops away from around me.

"Who did this to you?" So dangerous, that voice. "Who hurt you?"

"It's nothing."

The muscle in his jaw flexes. "These weren't on you last night. I didn't— I didn't hurt you?"

Oh gods. Relief shears through me. "No. It wasn't…. You didn't bruise me."

But someone did, his eyes say.

"It's nothing."

"Did *she* do this?" There's murder in his eyes, and it's a shock to realize he would kill my mother for daring to touch me.

I can't breathe all of a sudden.

The last person who tried to protect me was tortured and cast from the castle. After Nanny Redwyne disappeared, I swore I'd never let myself love another person again.

But holding your emotions at bay means withdrawing from the world.

Maybe that's why I'm so vulnerable to his touch. Maybe it's because a part of me is do desperate to *be* touched.

"It's nothing," I repeat. "I… I did the wrong thing."

Thiago visibly swallows down his fury. "I have no right to ask. I have no right to... protect you." He hates the thought, I can tell. Sliding his fingers through mine, he lifts my hand once more, pressing a gentle kiss to the back of it. "I have no right to even tell you what you should and shouldn't do. You're not mine." His voice roughens. "You can never me mine. But if there is one thing I know it is this—you deserve to be treated with respect. There's nothing you could have done to have earned this, and whoever set hands to you in anger deserves to be fucking flogged. You deserve better—"

I press my finger to his lips because I can't bear to hear more. "I know I deserve better," I tell him fiercely. "But wishes don't come true."

There's an ancient pain in his eyes. "Maybe they could?"

"Then grant me this wish. Give me one more night," I whisper, stroking my fingertips over the stubble lining his jaw. "Whatever this madness is, let me have it just one more time. Kiss me. Please."

Thiago's eyes turn molten.

But this time, he gently traces my cheek as he leans toward me. "If I'm only going to have you one more time, then I can't waste a moment of it."

His lips brush mine.

It's not a claim this time.

It's a seduction.

I hadn't realized until this moment that a kiss could be both. It feels like he's trying to do this right, and make up for the passion that overtook the both of us last night. I could kiss him forever. He's good at this, and I don't think that's my inexperience showing.

Tiny shivers erupt over my skin as his tongue darts out to taste my lips. I want to step into him, to press myself against every inch of him, but something inside me wants this moment too.

My mouth opens and I stroke his tongue with mine. Thiago shudders and that feels good too, because I'm not the only one being seduced in this moment. It gives me a heady kind of power. I dig my nails into his forearms and lift onto my toes, claiming his mouth. *Mine.* It's a thrill that runs all the way through me, curling like a warm heat within my core.

"I want to see you naked," I whisper, drawing back and staring up at him through glazed eyes. "I want to touch you. I want to taste you."

He sucks in a sharp breath. "Gods, it's like you were made for me."

Capturing me in his arms, he takes two steps and then lays me down upon the heather. I grab a fistful of his shirt and haul him down atop me, his hips sliding between my welcoming thighs.

He crawls up the length of me, the weight of his body driving me onto my back as his mouth finds my throat. Teeth graze against sensitive skin. I'm burning up. Desperate. My hands grip the heavy muscle of his upper arms, but I don't know if I'm trying to hold on, or demand some space between us—just enough to breathe.

Every inch of me erupts in shivers from the tight, swollen ache of my nipples, to the pulsing wetness between my thighs.

Wrong. So wrong.

There's no denying the truth now.

I can't pretend I don't know who he is anymore.

I can't pretend I'm not taking this step willfully.

And I can't pretend I don't want this with every inch of my body.

"More," I pant.

Capturing my chin, Thiago claims my mouth. His tongue pushes past my lips. A muscular knee forces my thighs apart, and then it's grinding against my pussy. Sucking in a sharp gasp behind my teeth, I dig my nails into his arms. All that muscle, just for me. I want to bite him. I want to eat him alive. I want those powerful hands on my skin. I want pain. I want pleasure. I want him inside me so desperately I can barely breathe.

It's like he reads my mind.

His lips trail down the smooth column of my throat, hands tugging at the filmy gauze of my dress. One breast is bared and then his mouth is there, molten with heat. I arch into him and he suckles me into his mouth. *More. More.* It feels like wildfire ignites within my veins.

"I want to never let you go," he whispers, his eyes meeting mine.

"Then don't."

The words set him loose.

If I thought the possessive claim in his eyes was over-whelming before, then I knew nothing.

Hands tear at my skirts, ripping the expensive silk. I arch into his palm as he finds me, wet and slick. Two fingers drive inside me and I nearly scream. He's kissing me again. Hard. Furious. Desperate. It feels like we're both fighting for breath, as if the air in his lungs is all that can sustain me.

His thumb works over me, his fingers driving in and out in a pistoning movement. *Oh gods*. A storm is brewing.

"You're so fucking tight." He bites my throat. "Come for me, Vi. Give me your pleasure."

One simple command and I'm coming all over his fingers with a scream. This time I give into temptation and bite his shoulder. It's a million times more heady than it was last night. I can't control myself.

I don't want to control myself.

Collapsing against the grass, I shake and shudder. Thiago reaches over his shoulder, tugging his tunic over his head. He casts it aside and I rear up on my elbows to look. Shadow ripples over his muscles, delineating them with an artist's touch. He's perfect. All hard muscle and smooth skin. Thick dark tattoos that smolder over his chest. I try to run my fingers over one and I swear it moves, arching beneath my touch like a cat.

Thiago captures my hand.

"If you keep looking at me like that, Vi, this is going to be over before we even begin." He tears the buttons on his leather trousers open, unleashing that monstrous cock.

I know it fits—I *know*—but the sight of it knots me up inside. For all the pleasure last night brought, there was also a little pain. Understandable, of course, but….

"Don't be nervous," he whispers, fisting that brute and gliding his hand up and down in a mesmerizing movement. Cum glistens over the slit of his cock. He dashes it off with his thumb, and then brings it to my lips.

I suckle hard, the taste surprisingly salty.

Our eyes meet, and then he's cursing under his breath, settling himself between my thighs. "You test my patience each and every time. Fuck, Vi. I wanted to seduce you tonight."

The head of his cock brushes against me. I shiver, long past the need for seduction. "We don't have time for that."

I need to be back before someone realizes I'm missing.

"There's always time."

I grab his ass in both hands, but he refuses to sink into me. Instead he traces those teasing fingers between my thighs. Lightning strikes twice. I come with a moan, shamelessly grinding into his touch.

"You're so responsive," he whispers. "I love it."

Resting on one elbow, he fits himself to me and I brace for impact, but once again he surprises me.

He makes shallow thrusts, dipping inside an inch and then retreating. Messy fingers trace slick circles over and around my clit. I'd accuse him of missing the mark, but one look into those eyes reveals he knows exactly what he's doing.

Locking my thighs around his lean hips, I try to arch into him on the next stroke and earn an extra inch.

A dangerous smile curls over his mouth. "Do you want me, Vi?"

"Oh gods." A moan escapes me. *Yes. Please.* He's driving me to the edge again with each supple stroke, that callused thumb flickering over my clit just enough to make me gasp. Wild with need. Desperate to have him inside me. "Are you just a fucking tease?"

"Mmm." The smoky sound curls all the way through me as he nuzzles at my throat. "Always. I like it when you beg. I like it when you gasp my name. I like it" —he sinks inside me further, his thumb pressing hard against my clit — "when you scream."

His thumb should be immortalized. There should be a statue of it in some hall somewhere. I can't escape the pressure of it, and it feels like it unlocks something inside me.

"*Thiago.*"

"Just. Like. That." His voice is a whisper inside my head, conjuring memories and fantasies. "Maybe I'll fuck you with my tongue instead. Would you like that, Vi? Right here." His cock retreats, teasing at me, testing me. I can almost imagine his tongue doing this dance.

Another inch.

If he doesn't fill me right now, I'm going to explode.

"*Please,*" I gasp.

"Please, what?"

"Please *fuck* me."

Grasping my thighs, he drives into me with one smooth stroke. It's enough to tip me over the edge and I do scream. I can barely handle it as he thrusts within me. Harder and faster. Pinning my wrists above my head, and then capturing my thigh and shoving it higher so he's sinking so deep within me I can barely breathe.

"Thiago." I moan again. Surely my body can't handle this much pleasure.

"Vi." He rests his forehead against mine, his thrusts slowing and the muscles in his throat cording. It's beautiful to see his surrender. There's no kindness in it. Indeed, it looks like pain as he throws his head back and gasps, flexing one more time.

But the peace that floods across his expression afterward....

I'll remember that.

No matter what happens, I will always remember this moment.

Thiago slumps heavily against me, breathing hard as he withdraws. The slickness of his seed paints my thigh, and he traces his fingers through it as if the sensation of it gives him some sort of possessive pleasure.

I curl into his arms, resting my head on his shoulder. My dress is tangled around me. His trousers are still wrapped around one of his ankles. It makes me laugh and Thiago lifts his head to see what amuses me.

"What?"

"You keep breaking your promises," I tease. "You said tonight would be slow, but we could barely wait until we were undressed."

A smile touches his mouth. It's the first one I've truly seen and its breathtaking. It feels like the sun rises within him, casting away the shadows of night. He's dangerously handsome at all times, but right now, I think he could steal my heart.

"What is it?" he asks, as if sensing the sudden panic that spirals through me.

"Nothing."

Thiago slumps back down, but his hand runs along my hip. "You say that a lot, you know?"

I go still, my heart beating fast. It's an easy way to hide my heart, but maybe I need to stop doing that. "I like your smile."

He rolls me onto my side, so he can see me.

"Do you?" he whispers as we stare into each other's eyes. There's a dangerous sense of longing within him. "You make me smile. Even when I know I shouldn't."

Further confirmation that this only lasts until dawn.

I close my eyes and kiss him again. "I like all the things I shouldn't be doing with you."

"Really?" His answer is a rough laugh as he takes my hand and curls my fingers through his.

"But I almost think I like this the best," I whisper as we hold each other.

It's a tremulous admission.

I trace his arms, his shoulders, those tattoos. As wonderful as the fucking is, it's this moment that truly threatens me. I know he feels it too. He's too still, too thoughtful. And his chest rises and falls in steady increments as if he barely dares break the truce between us.

But then he does.

"I wish that I could trust in you," Thiago whispers. There's a storm in his eyes, and he captures my surprise on my lips. One long heated kiss that steals my breath. Then he's kissing my cheeks, my nose. "But I can't help thinking that you were never meant to be a gift. You were meant to be my destruction."

The moment is gone, a portentous shiver running through me. "Don't say that."

His eyes darken. I almost don't recognize the look in them. "There's almost a part of me that doesn't care. Shatter me, Vi. Break me. Destroy me. I will love every moment of it, until we crash and burn."

I shove him onto his back and then sling my legs over

his hips. Pressing a finger to his lips, I shake my head. "Stop saying that. Stop tempting fate."

"You don't believe in fate."

I shiver, and he smiles.

"Fate already fucked me once," he whispers, his thumbs rasping up the outside of my thighs. "It can wait its turn. Maybe we can make our own fate."

And then he flexes up and kisses me again, drawing me down to our ruin.

8

ISKVIEN

I wish that I could trust in you....

The words spin around my head as I circle my small tent the following day.

I slept with the Prince of Evernight. Again.

It's almost like I have some sort of weakness for arrogant, handsome males who are nothing like they seem to be on the surface.

But I can't help thinking that Thiago and Etan are worlds apart.

Thiago was angry yesterday. Furious with the reveal of my identity.

And yet, not once did I ever feel threatened.

It's a heady realization.

The evil Prince of Evernight—the one who murdered his queen and her heirs, the one who seeks to steal my mother's rightful lands away from her—wanted to know why I have bruises on my wrists.

I pace and I pace and I pace.

There are thoughts churning in my mind. Dangerous thoughts.

I can see him again, the backs of his knuckles brushing against my cheek as our eyes meet, and he sinks deep inside me. I can feel my breath catching, feel that moment branding itself on my skin. Taste his kiss on my lips as he stills and lets me adjust to his size and weight.

It's all starting to merge in my mind.

My mother digs the knife into the skin beneath Finn's eye.

My hands shake as I sign the contract that will bind me to a monster.

And Thiago's mouth captures mine as he hauls me against him, and I wilt into his arms, wanting nothing more than to lose myself in him.

I promised my mother I would sign the marriage contract.

I never promised her I would go through with the marriage.

"Fuck it." I'm moving before I can think my way through the entire plot. The problem is this Finn. If I renege, she'll kill him. Painfully.

But if he's no longer here....

Then she can't do a cursed thing to him.

And I heard the pain in Thiago's voice last night.

If I can do nothing else for him, then I can give him this: I can set his friend free.

There's no one in my mother's tent right now, thanks to a private meeting with the queens of Aska and Ravenal, and I know the guard's rotations. Edain will be with my mother to serve as her personal protector. Andraste will be sitting on a cushion by her knee, smiling as she drinks down their wine and their threats.

The Asturian guards are good.

They know they can't afford to allow my mother's precious hostage to escape.

But they're not looking for an attack on the inside.

No, they're looking toward the tents of Evernight or Stormlight.

I need a cloak, I need a knife, maybe some of those hair pins that I learned to pick a lock with, and gloves, for the iron. Half a minute later I have everything I need and then I'm slipping from the tent and pulling the hood of my cloak over my dark hair.

Night's not far away. More bonfires. Middenmarch tonight. We will sing to the ancestors who fled to this world, and burn the pyres to remember them. Blessed Maia. Blessed Selena. Blessed Ambryn.

This is the night the queens plot.

This is the night accords are made, and treaties formed.

Nobody will be looking for me. I'm in disgrace with my mother. Forgotten. Barely watched.

I count to three as a guard strolls past, wait until he's around the corner of the tents, and then I slip into the shadows. Five seconds later, I'm inside my mother's tent.

A single torch burns. Veils of fine linen hang to separate rooms within the tent.

My mother's bed is opulent—all red and gold cushions, with fine silk sheets and furs cast there.

Edain's chambers settle off hers, with a neat pallet laid out on the floor. It barely looks used.

There's a cage within his chambers, a shadowy figure curled up on the floor within it. I ease through the linens, pressing a finger to my lips as Finn's eyes blink open in surprise.

It's dark back here. I can see the shadowy figure of a guard pass by outside, carrying a torch.

Finn peers at me through his sweat-dampened hair, straining to see who just entered. His eyes widen in recognition and he opens his mouth, before he sees my finger. His mouth closes, but his surprise remains apparent.

The torch fades. The guard walks away. We're as alone as we're ever going to be, and we have three minutes until the next guard circles around.

A heavy iron ring circles his neck, and someone's bolted it to the side of his cage.

Iron. This might be a problem.

I can pick a lock, but even touching those bars will burn my hands. The gloves will help, but iron seems to emanate with its poison and though my tolerance for it is higher than most, I'm not entirely immune.

"Well," Finn says in a roughened whisper as I circle the cage. "I can't say I expected to see *you* here. Princess, was it? Princess Iskvien?"

"Be quiet." I kneel down. There's a lock on the cage, and I'm sure the key is hidden somewhere in Edain's chambers, but the problem lies with what I can't see.

The cage will be warded.

The second I touch that lock, the owner of the ward will know about it. The question is, did my mother lay that trap? Or was it Edain?

How fast can they return?

And why the hell does my magic elude me? If I'd been able to wield it, I might have been able to break these wards with none the wiser.

"What are you doing?" Finn sits up, frowning a little.

"Isn't it obvious? I'm rescuing you."

Apparently, it isn't obvious, because his eyebrows almost meet his hairline. I study the lock and then realize those gorgeous blue eyes are searching my face.

"What?" I whisper.

There are shadows in his expression. "What's the cost of this, Princess?"

"There is no cost. Not to you."

He captures my wrist through the bars, moving shockingly fast. "I'm not talking about me. I saw and heard everything your mother did yesterday." He shakes his head. "I always knew she was a bitch, but I didn't realize she treated her own family like that."

I wrench my hand back.

There's a gaping wound in my chest, an emptiness I can't fill. It's one thing to know that my mother despises me, but another to have others see it.

He pities me. My enemy pities me.

"It doesn't matter," I whisper, and then try to force a smile. "It won't be the first time she hurts me. It won't be the last." And then there's the matter of this marriage to Etan. *What's the worst thing she can do to me when she's fucking selling me to a monster?*

A hand curls around mine and I realize I slipped away for a moment.

He's watching me. Eyes full of sympathy.

"I'm Finn," he says, as if he's not locked in a cage barely big enough to house a dog.

"I know."

His smile curves, slightly wicked. "I figured a formal introduction might be in order, considering you're rescuing me. It's a little embarrassing, after all."

"Embarrassing?" The word draws me out of the emptiness.

He shrugs, muscle moving in his chest and shoulders. "I'm the one who's usually rescuing princesses."

He has an easy charm about him that makes me relax.

"Do tell…. Ever tried to pick a lock?" I ask.

"Frequently." He nudges the door of the cage with his boot. "Not this one though. Not yet."

"The lock will be warded," I murmur. "If anyone touches it…."

"It will summon a wrathful prince," he says with a wink. "Want to know a secret, Princess?"

I arch a brow.

Finn slowly reaches out and grips the lock in both hands, gritting his teeth with pain as the iron burns through him.

But nothing happens.

Both of us breathe out as he lets go.

"I kept grabbing the lock in the first day," he says with a smile. "Having that ward blare in his head like a horn every hour or two was annoying him. So he altered the ward."

Finn can touch the lock without summoning Edain.

"I just need something to pick it with."

I reach inside my pocket and produce my catch.

Finn eyes my hairpin with barely disguised disdain.

"It works," I tell him. "I've done it many a time."

"On what? Your bedchambers?"

Maybe.

"Over there," he says, tipping his head toward Edain's pallet and the piles of saddlebags there. "His Royal Sulkiness put the key in there."

I scramble across the floor toward the packs.

"But you're not going to touch the key," Finn whispers. "It's a trap. I saw him lay the magic on it. Something violent, by the look of it. No. What you're looking for is a satchel of knives. He's got an entire roll of them. There's a dirk there. Thin enough to stab through an ear without leaving a mark."

I arch a brow at that and find the satchel. "Plotting your escape, were you?"

A flash of a smile greets me. "Not my first time in a cage, Princess. Nor my last, I daresay. Though I wasn't expecting a helpful accomplice to simply amble in here, and hadn't yet figured out how to get my hands on that dirk."

I find the dirk.

The hilt of every single knife in that roll of leather is carved of something pale, like ivory. Or bone. The hilts are gold. The blades wickedly sharp. But the dirk is a thing of murderous beauty.

This was only ever created for assassination.

I know Edain works in the shadows.

There have been slips of the tongue over the years— mostly my mother—and enemies who simply... vanished. Or were found in their beds with their throats expertly cut.

"Here," I whisper as I hand it over with the gloves. "These might help."

"Thanks." He tugs the gloves on, and leans as close to the cage door as he can with the collar around his neck. Absolute focus settles over his expression as he begins to work the dirk inside the lock.

"Can I... Can I ask you a question?"

A little notch draws between his brows as he tries to slip the tumblers. "I'm not married, sweetheart, but alas, my heart's already spoken for."

A nervous laugh tears from me. He's ridiculous. But somehow it gives me the strength to say this. "You work for the Prince of Evernight."

This time he looks up. "Yes."

"What's he... like?"

A dozen expressions flicker over his face as if I came at him from a direction he didn't expect. "Thiago?"

I wait.

"Oh, I see now." His smile turns into a shit-eating grin. "I thought all of this recklessness was for me, but you caught a glimpse of my prince, didn't you? My poor broken heart."

Heat scours my cheeks. "Your heart's already spoken for."

"I lied." He shrugs. "I do that on occasion." He looks far too interested in the topic at hand. "And you're not going to distract me now. Tell me everything."

"There's nothing to tell." My cheeks flame. "I just... wanted to know. Whether he was... kind?"

"Kind?" Finn tests the word. "He is strict. With himself," he clarifies, when my gaze jerks to his. "It's not kindness, so much as protectiveness. He'll kill to save those he considers his own. And he has all these sorts of rules for himself that nobody, least of all me, can understand. But he'd never hurt an innocent. He's loyal, and proud, and aloof, and—"

"Aloof?" That wasn't at all the impression I gained.

Finn sighs. "Sometimes there's a darkness within him. A distance. You'll see him staring out over the city as if he sees something else, and you can speak his name but he's not there. And then it's like he breaks free of the trance, or shatters the hold of whatever's got him distracted, and then he'll blink and *he's* back. The prince I know. The prince I've fought side-by-side with. The prince I love."

Love. It's such a strange word to hear from a male's mouth like that.

Finn chuckles. "Not like that, Princess. He's my brother, in the way that we chose to be family. I love him. I will kill for him. I will die for him. And I will set this world on fire if it tries to hurt him."

I hate that I'm envious of that. I can't remember the last time I knew such a concept.

No. I do. I remember my childhood with Andraste. Fingers clasped around a tree as we danced in circles around it, singing '*The oaks fall down, the oaks fall down....*'

Laughing and giggling with her as we rolled in the grass and picked daisies, turning them into crowns we placed on each other's heads.

I would have died to protect that. To protect her.

But then the night came when Mother caught Nanny Redwyne reading stories to us from the book she'd banned. Stories of the old creatures who ruled Arcaedia before the fae arrived.

The Green Man that made the lands of Asturia bloom long before my mother's ancestors came to power. Bloody Mara, who protects women against all who prey on them, and whose name could be called three times when one was in need. The Erlking, who ruled the fearful Wild Hunt which rode the forests on Samhain, and yet who could be appealed upon for his justice. His mercy.

Wondrous tales of ancient creatures that made me terribly curious about those who lived here before the fae.

Forbidden tales.

And I asked for them. I begged and Nanny hesitated, but eventually she gave in and slipped the book into my room of nights, where she'd hide it beneath my mattress during the day.

Until my mother suddenly appeared in the door one night, as if she'd been waiting for precisely this moment.

"Since you heed not my royal proclamations," my mother had hissed as her guards pinned Nanny to the ground, *"then it seems I must ensure they are heard by all who see you. Your eyes shall never read such blasphemy again. Your tongue shall not proclaim it. And your ears will not hear it."*

And then she made me watch as Nanny screamed and screamed and screamed while the soldiers removed those offending pieces of her.

That was the night I knocked over a candle and nearly burned half the tower down.

That was the night my fledgling magic snuffed itself out.

135

And that was the night Andraste was torn away from me, our lessons separated, our rooms moved to opposing wings of the castle.

That was the night my mother first looked at me with cold disdain.

The last time I dared love someone—the last time I was *loved*—was eight years ago now.

"Hey." A gentle hand curls over mine. "Are you okay?"

I let go of the breath I've been holding, tears pricking in my eyes. "I was just thinking about... what it would be like to live in a kingdom where you could trust your ruler."

Finn bites his lip. It feels weird to be holding hands like this with a stranger in the darkened chambers of my mother's tent. It feels strange to trust him.

But I do.

Instantly.

Even more so than I trusted Thiago—perhaps because Thiago represents a seductive threat to me on some level, whereas Finn is simply... a charming stranger. A likeable stranger.

"I can kidnap you when I leave," he says. "Put my knife against your throat and drag you out of here and make it clear you're not coming with me of your own voli-tion." There's a sudden twinkle in his eyes. "Maybe it will give you a chance to see if my prince is 'kind' enough for you."

"That sounds like a terrible plan."

"But you're tempted—"

I don't know what it is that alerts me, because there's

no noise. But I have a sudden, wretched feeling we're no longer alone.

"Stay still. Don't move. Don't say anything," I hiss in his ear, stealing the dirk from his hands.

"What's going on?"

I scramble through a slit in the canvas walls, finding myself in what appears to be Mother's wardrobe. Slipping beneath the enormous drape of the skirt on one of her dresses, I crouch low and peek out from under the hem.

Finn clearly realizes what I'm doing because he strips the gloves off and sits on them.

Just in time.

The tent flaps fling open and an enormous shadow appears.

Edain.

My stepbrother freezes in the opening to this section of the tent, his gaze raking the shadows. Every inch of him is coiled with tension; a predator just waiting to strike. Just my luck. He may have changed the wards on the cage, but something must have set them off.

"What's wrong, pretty boy?" Finn taunts abruptly. "Come to find your balls? I believe your queen has them locked away in a chest in her room."

Edain cuts him a look and then stalks inside, his shadow rippling over the walls as he lifts his torch high. "Who's been in here?"

"Me and all my merry friends."

Through the linen, I see Edain's lip curl in frustration as he sets the torch in its ring. "Someone was picking the lock on your cage. I set wards within it."

Finn holds up a hair pin. "Can't blame a lad for trying."

Edain snatches it. "Where did you get this?"

"Have you seen the elaborate coiffures your queen wears?" Finn gives him an arrogant look. "Maybe you didn't notice when she shook them from her hair last night, but I did."

Edain lashes through the cage and grabs a fistful of his shirt. He swiftly pats him down.

"Here now," Finn protests. "A man likes a little sweet talk first." He flinches as Edain's hands slide through his back pockets. "The real weapon's in the front."

Edain freezes.

Their faces are inches from each other, and I'm trying not to breathe under my nest of skirts.

Fuck. This is awkward.

They stare at each other through the bars on the cage, and then Finn shivers. "Stop looking at me like that, Pet. Your queen wouldn't approve if she caught you feeling me up like a lecherous barmaid."

"Maybe I should have let her whip you bloody," Edain says in disgust as he sinks back onto his knees. "You have a mouth on you."

"Oh, I do." They're still staring at each other. "Want to try it?"

Finn bursts out laughing as Edain shoves to his feet, scrubbing at his mouth.

"I'm starting to realize why your prince hasn't made a counteroffer yet," Edain says. "Maybe he doesn't want you back. Maybe we've done him a favor."

It cuts through Finn's laughter. "My prince doesn't negotiate with blackmailers."

"How's that make you feel?" Edain sneers. "You're worthless to him."

Finn merely crosses his legs and rests his hands on his thighs. "I know my worth," he says simply. "Do you?"

There's a stillness within Edain. For all that he appears to hold the upper hand, I can see Finn scored first blood.

"Whether you know your own worth or not," he finally says, "if your prince doesn't give us what we want, then she will kill you. Slowly. Painfully."

"You mean she'll make *you* kill me. Slowly. Painfully."

Edain gives him a long, heated look.

Finn sighs. "You hate it, don't you? What's she have on you?"

Bleakness darkens my stepbrother's face. "Everything."

"Then why don't you—"

"Edain?"

The sound of his name echoes through the enormous tent.

I freeze as I recognize my sister's voice.

But curiously enough, so does Edain. His head tracks toward the sound, all his attention focusing upon her. "Andraste?"

"Maybe your intruder was a princess herself," Finn taunts. "Maybe she wanted to know what a real male looks like."

I can't see my stepbrother's response, but I can feel Finn tense as if he's waiting for a blow. "Keep your mouth shut about our princess," Edain finally says. "And don't tempt me."

"Let me out of the cage, pretty princeling, and maybe we can dance again. We can wrestle a little bit more. I wonder though, who will end up on top?" Everything about the way he says the words is suggestive. "This time you won't have the element of surprise."

Edain stalks toward the door. "I won't need it."

And then he's gone in a swirl of canvas, and my heart is suddenly beating like the galloping of a horse's hooves. Close. Too close.

If he'd found me in here, then my mother would be furious.

What am I doing?

It makes no sense. None of this makes any sense.

Breathe. I ease the breath from my lungs and force my hands to stop shaking.

"Well, that was interesting," Finn says in some surprise. "Your boy likes cock as much as he likes sweet pussy. I thought he was almost going to take me up on my offer."

I grind my teeth together as I crawl out from beneath the dress and then slip back into Edain's chambers. "The things I do not need to know."

Finn laughs under his breath. "You know, you almost sound exactly like my prince right now."

Our eyes meet. He's picking at me as much as he picked at Edain. It would be easy to dismiss him for a rogue, but there's a cunning intelligence in those blue eyes. He knows exactly what he's doing.

"Now *that's* interesting," Finn breathes, as I return to

the lock. "You never did tell me how you met my prince, but here's that blush again, stealing up your cheeks. I'm shattered, truly. I thought we were starting to get to know each other."

"You were *just* flirting with my stepbrother."

"Distraction, sweetheart. I was channeling my inner Lysander. And don't change the subject. Have you kissed Thiago?"

I ignore him. How are we going to manage this? "He put the ward inside the lock itself."

"Ah yes, but the ward is broken. I was trying to distract him so he didn't reset it." Finn steals the dirk from me, jams it inside and after a few playful twists the lock clicks. "And you did, you naughty girl. Where did you kiss him?"

His eyes light up as the cage door swings open.

"Like I'd tell you." I drive the point of the dirk into the tiny screw that binds his collar together.

"On the mouth?" He laughs as I grumble under my breath. "That's a yes. Did you kiss him anywhere else, Iskvien?"

I swear, I could just about wring his neck myself.

The collar gives way, and Finn shoves forward, scrambling out the cage. He takes a step and winces. "Bastard shot me with an arrow when he took me down. It's nearly healed, but it might take the edge off me."

I cross my arms. "I *could* help you."

"Could?"

"Only if you promise not to ask me any more questions about kissing. We still have to escape this quadrant of the camp without being seen, and return you to your prince."

"Oh, princess." Finn stretches his arms behind his

141

back, his spine cracking. "That's the easy part. I've had loads of experience in escaping traps. The hard part comes when your mother realizes I'm gone and starts to wonder how I managed it." He shoots me a brilliant smile as I slip under his shoulder. "And I promise on my life that I won't ask you any more questions about my prince. I already know the answers, and I can't *wait* to see what Eris thinks of you."

9

THIAGO

"Let us start," Adaia purrs, as she crosses one long smooth leg over the other, her golden metallic skirts falling apart to reveal the slit. "I have something you want. Now I want to know how much you want it back."

I stare at her and I can see Vi's bruises again. And the way she tried to hide them.

And I know what that little smirk is telling me about Finn's condition.

Everything within me yearns to wipe it from Adaia's face, but we're playing at diplomacy now, and Lucidia is watching.

The ancient queen of Ravenal is the only true neutral vote on the Seelie Alliance. Kyrian sides with me and Maren most commonly with Adaia.

It is to her that we bring this dispute.

"I'm sure you do," I murmur, "but Evernight has neither proof of Finn's life or condition, and before we begin, I intend to have it."

"I give you my word," Adaia states. "He is alive and he is well."

This time it's my turn to smile. "You think I would ever believe you at your word?"

"Adaia speaks the truth," Lucidia confirms. "I was brought to see your man not one-hour past. He is in reasonable condition and alive."

Reasonable fucking condition. I know what that means.

"Don't look at me like that," Lucidia chides.

"I want to know if he's been tortured." The muscle in my jaw twitches.

"He is alive," Adaia snaps.

Lucidia arches a brow toward her. "I've seen no signs of torture, though I do believe a whip was used upon him."

A whip. I am going to kill this bitch with my own fucking hands. One day.

Take her apart piece by piece, whispers Ruin.

Break every bone in her body, says Wrath. *Her screams would be music.*

Of all the Darkyn souls I've consumed, he's the most violent.

I lean forward in my chair. "Then why don't we see—?"

Eris's hand comes to rest upon my shoulder. "A word?" she whispers.

This is the worst possible time for it, but I cut her a look. She wouldn't make this demand unless there was something important she needed to tell me. She knows how much Finn's life rests on a knife edge.

I nod, and she passes me a slip of folded paper.

The words inside are Thalia's.

We have Finn. Don't give that bitch anything.

We also have something else you might be interested in.

—T

We have Finn. Something inside me unknots. I came here willing to barter my soul for my brother-in-arms. It's the promise I made to myself when Finn, Baylor, Lysander, and Thalia backed me when I took the throne. I will always have their backs—because I know they have mine.

This is my family.

It's the one thing I've managed to forge for myself that can't be taken away.

That *won't* be taken away, no matter what I have to do.

"Well?" Adaia leans back in her chair, her smile small and tight. It's the smile of a queen certain she's about the make her enemy crawl. There's nothing of Vi in that smile. It seems a miracle that this snake bred a daughter like her. "What say you? Mistmere in exchange for your misplaced hunter?"

I meet her gaze and it's truly a pleasure to smile a "fuck you" in her direction. "I say no." Pushing to my feet, I give Lucidia a brief nod. "Thank you for agreeing to reconcile both our kingdoms. But I will no longer be needing your services."

Adaia gapes at me. "Thiago?"

I push to my feet and smile toward her. "Maybe we will meet again one day soon. But you should look to your own people. Just where did your pet vanish to in such a rush?"

And I leave her with the possibility that I've made my own counterattack.

~

"WHAT DOES THALIA MEAN BY 'SOMETHING ELSE I MIGHT be interested in?'" I duck beneath the canvas flap of the ornate tent that bears my colors.

Eris strides along in my wake, one hand resting on the hilt of her sword. We crossed the campgrounds in under a minute, but it's never wise to speak too loudly outside. Thalia's had my tent warded nine ways to the Underworld, and the second we're inside, the curiosity gets the better of me.

Thalia shoves to her feet, her shoulders slumping in relief as I enter. "Tell me we reached you in time. Tell me you signed none of her demands."

"You reached me in time. I've given her nothing." I rest a hand on her shoulder. "Now where is Finn?"

"Currently enjoying Evernight hospitality once again." Finn emerges from a side chamber, his hair wet and a towel hanging around his broad neck. He's lost weight and he's rubbing cream into his ruined wrists, but the relief I feel is instantaneous.

He's not dead.

"You look like shit," he tells me.

Really? "You're one to speak."

Curse him. I wrench him into a hug and slap his shoulder gently, squeezing tight. I was the one who sent him to Mistmere. I wanted to know what Adaia was doing sending her people sniffing around the ancient Hallow, and

I sent him directly into a trap. If she'd killed him— "You weren't supposed to get caught."

Finn grins at me as I let him go. "It's a long story," he protests. "A dashing ruin. A moonlit tower. An ambush. Half a dozen wolfhounds. Maybe an entire company of Asturian soldiers and—"

"Perhaps we can give him the short version?" Eris mutters. "The Lammastide rites end in twenty-four hours."

"Fine. I fled. The wolfhounds gave chase. Someone put an arrow through my fucking calf, and they were on me before I could even get up." Finn shrugs.

"I thought you were the most dangerous warrior to grace the north," Eris says with a snort. "A mere flesh wound shouldn't aggravate you so."

Shadows darken Finn's eyes for all of a second. "I didn't say it was a warrior who put that arrow in me." There's trouble in his eyes when he looks at me. "The queen's pet was the one who took me down. He blew a fistful of powder in my face and the next thing I knew, I was shackled in the back of a wagon. One at my throat, both wrists, both ankles. I may as well have been in a pillory, and the fucker used iron. Not even I can break that apart."

"The queen's pet? Her stepson?" I've seen Edain from across the gathering, all silk and velvet and dark hair pomaded back from his face. An insolent leopard lounging at Adaia's feet, though judging from the golden collar around his throat, he's leashed.

There's no way he's good enough to take Finn down.

Finn is part-Sylvaren: the warrior-born.

"The queen's assassin most likely." Finn rubs the towel

through his hair. He shakes his head at me. "Don't mistake him for Adaia's whore. That bastard doesn't fight fairly. He doesn't have to. He's got enough tricks up his sleeve to keep *me* on my knees, and he barely had to twitch a finger."

"If I rip his head off," Baylor growls, "then he won't get a chance."

"Aye, but you'd have to get close enough," Finn counters, shaking a finger at the enormous general.

Lysander sighs. "It's always the pretty ones you've got to watch. Maybe I can take a tilt at him? He won't even see me coming."

"I don't think so," Finn mutters. "He's good."

Lysander grins. "You never know. He and I shared a moment when we both tried to stalk through the arch to the queensmoot at the same time. He looked like he wanted to murder me. Someone's repressing all his worst impulses...."

"If Edain's repressing anything," Finn says, "it's violence. Don't put yourself at risk. I doubt either you or Baylor could take him. Besides...." He tosses the towel to Eris, and then reaches for his shirt, hauling it over his shoulders gingerly. "If anyone's going to repay the queen's pet for her *kindness*, it's going to be me."

The sight of his back stalls all conversation.

I suck a hiss of air through my teeth, and Eris's hands clench in Finn's towel.

He looks up, his gaze wary.

"Erlking's hairy cock." The breeze wheezes through Eris's teeth as she forces Finn to still, easing the cotton of his shirt away from his skin. "What the fuck happened to you?"

She wasn't there when Lucidia announced what had been done to him.

"I'm fine."

Their eyes meet, and there's murder in Eris's expression. "You are not fine. Who did this?"

Finn shrugs. "Let us just say that the queen of Asturia has certain proclivities, and they involve a whip in her hand."

I turn Finn around and the sight of his back does things to me. The welts that remain are still raw. Dozens of them, crisscrossing his skin like mesh. Maybe even a hundred. I knew they were there, but knowing it doesn't mean it's easier to accept.

"I'm fine, Thiago," Finn says curtly. "Nothing that won't heal."

"These cut to the bone." There's a hollow rage inside me. She did this to him *because* of me.

"Most of the time, seeing a beautiful woman with a whip in her hand might make a man consider just how far he intends to allow matters to go, but I will admit Adaia's cured me of any such desires."

"Lean forward," I say gruffly.

His gaze cuts to mine. "I'm fine, Thi. They'll heal. They'll probably even be gone by sunrise."

He and his sylvaren blood. The fae heal ridiculously fast and can survive mortal wounds, but he comes from a race of fae that were magically transmogrified by their queen. Every ounce of his strength and power is magnified. His healing abilities are off the charts.

"Get Mariana in here," I snap at Baylor. "Now."

The healer's magic can fix this.

I breathe through the rage. "How did you escape?"

"I didn't." Finn's brow quirks and he turns to the side. "I was rescued by a maid most fair and gallant." His smile holds an edge. "I tried to woo her, but it seems she's taken somewhat of a shine to someone else. Princess?"

Thalia steps aside, and I finally realize there's someone else in the tent.

Iskvien sits primly in a small chair flanking the edge of the tent.

It's immediately clear she's the "something else".

"What are you doing here?" My heart kicks in my chest. Finn drops away. The rest of my people fade. We might as well be alone, because our eyes meet and she's all I see.

There's no hint of the laughter that stole my breath the first time we met. No sign of her soft smile, her sweetness, the shy way she looked up at me as I kissed her and drove her into the heather. *No.* This is the princess of Asturia.

Shoulders square as if she's facing the gallows. Chin raised as she stares me down. I finally see a hint of her mother about her expression, but there's a strength there that Adaia has never owned. This is defiance. This is reckless courage.

This is power.

It near takes my breath away.

"My mother was going to cut his head off and deliver it on a platter," she says, "when you arrived to exchange him for Mistmere. I didn't know he was yours until you told me. I didn't even know he was in the camp until yesterday."

"So you rescued him?"

I don't know what to say to that.

Neither does she, apparently. "I... It didn't seem right."

"Tell him the truth, Princess," Finn says. He plucks a platter from the table and offers her some of our finest grapes. "Adaia was trying to force Iskvien into an arranged marriage. She used me as the bargaining chip to force Iskvien to sign the marriage contracts."

Arranged marriage?

Over Adaia's dead body.

"To who?" There's a snarl in my voice. That fucking blond bastard from the dance floor.

Vi stills. "It doesn't matter."

"It fucking well does. Who?"

"Etan of the Goldenhills. Queen Maren's nephew," Finn says, then gives a shrug when Vi shoots him a furious glare. "He's my prince, sweetheart. And from the sounds of it, he's got a vested interest in this." A brilliant smile flashes over his face. "What *have* I missed?"

"Nothing," Vi says.

At the exact moment I say, "Everything." And then I continue. "What do you mean Adaia forced you to sign it? Is that what those bruises were about?"

"The pet interceded and pointed out that if Iskvien was bruised, Maren would want to know why." Finn's mouth twists. "So Adaia put a knife to my face and promised to cut out my eye if Vi didn't submit." He rests a hand on Vi's shoulder. "I never did say thank you for your bravery."

"It wasn't bravery." It discomforts her, I can see. "I just.... I couldn't...."

"I know," Finn says. "But that is where you are wrong. To show kindness and empathy in such a world is the bravest thing that one can do. I know she says it makes you weak, but I disagree. Those are the sort of qualities that a warrior will fight to the death for." He suddenly goes to his knee in front of her. "I owe you two boons. You fought for me when your mother threatened to harm me. And then you freed me, at considerable risk to your own skin. You have my life, Princess. Merely tell me what you desire and I shall make it happen."

I slowly ease out the breath of fury I contain.

Because Thalia is softening toward her, and I know that with Finn's recommendation she will now follow Vi as her queen. Lysander will welcome her with open arms.

Even Baylor will give a shrug and a gruff, "Fine."

Only Eris stares at the princess with her arms crossed over her chest. "This is going to end badly," she promises. "Rescuing Finn is one thing, but now what? We have Adaia's daughter in our tent and no matter what Iskvien claims, her mother will call it kidnapping." She meets my eyes. "She's not Finn, Thiago. She's not merely... a reputable servant. She's her daughter. Adaia will demand satisfaction. Iskvien has to be returned before Adaia can even notice she's missing."

It's the wisdom of a general who can see a war brewing.

But I cannot agree. "I want a word with her first."

Finn pushes to his feet, and Lysander helps steady him.

"Alone," I say softly.

Eris looks like a spitting tom faced with a vicious dog.

"And then you may return her," I promise.

"You have ten minutes," Eris warns.

Finn winces. "Our prince may need slightly longer than that, my love."

"Ten minutes." She stalks toward the tent flap. "If he's that desperate to have her, surely that's long enough."

Oh, she's furious all right.

But I wave the others out after her.

I'll deal with Eris's misgivings later.

"YOU SAVED HIM," I MURMUR AS SOON AS THE TENT IS empty. "Thank you."

Iskvien pushes to her feet as if sitting leaves her at a disadvantage now we're alone. "It was nothing."

"It wasn't nothing." I take her hand. "I was about to sacrifice any claim upon Mistmere. Instead, your mother is left with a hand of useless cards." My voice roughens. "Can she trace this back to you?"

"I don't think so. We weren't seen. Edain will suspect someone helped him, though I doubt he'll think of me." Iskvien bites her lip. "Nobody ever suspects *me*."

I capture her face in my hands. "Come to me if you think she knows. I'll protect you."

But Vi tears away from my grasp. "I didn't just do it for you. She was holding him over my head. Now I'm free."

"To break this marriage contract?" I hate those words. To even think she's being forced to marry another....

She hesitates. "Yes."

My eyes narrow at the tone of voice used. That wasn't an emphatic "yes". Our eyes meet. "You don't have to marry him."

"If not Finn then it will be someone else," she says with a shrug. "My maid perhaps. My groom. She'll put a knife to their throat and force my hand and—"

"No." I slide a hand through her hair. "You do *not* have to marry him."

Fury suddenly blazes in her expression. "And how do I avoid such a fate?"

"By marrying *me*."

The words simply force their way past my lips.

Vi freezes.

Even I can't believe I just said it.

But the second I put them into the world, I know they're real.

This has been where my heart has been heading from the moment I laid eyes upon her.

I stroke my thumb over her satiny cheek. "Marry me," I whisper. "Be mine, Vi. She'll never be able to harm you again."

"As tempting as that is," she whispers, "I barely know you."

"You trusted me with your body."

She pushes away, pacing through the tent. "I *know*."

"Then why doubt me now?"

"How do I know that this hasn't been planned from the start?" A look that slays me. "I want to trust you. I want to believe this is real. But it's one thing to kiss you and lie with you, and quite another to bind my fate to yours." She

154

swallows. "This is forever, Thiago. And I can't help thinking about the war between you and my mother. I can't help thinking that you would do *anything* to destroy her." Her voice grows very small. "What if this was your plan from the start? Ruin me. Woo me. Steal me away."

"This has nothing to do with Adaia. *We* have nothing to do with her—"

She ducks beneath my arm as I reach for her. "There is no "we"." Frustration roars to life in her eyes. "Prove it. Prove that marrying me has nothing to do with spiting my mother. Prove this is real."

"And how do I do *that*?" When she won't believe my words.

She looks as though a thought occurs.

A horrible, terrible thought, judging by the way her cheeks pale.

"Give her the lands she wants," she says breathlessly. "Give her the territories in Mistmere. Do it and I'll marry you. Do it and I'll become your wife."

She may as well have struck me.

Give Adaia Mistmere?

No. A thousand times no. Not only is it dangerous politically, but it's become the playing piece I won't surrender. My pride won't allow it.

"You were willing to give it for Finn," she whispers.

If it was the only way I could save his life….

A part of me hates that she's asking this of me. A part of me applauds it. I don't want just a wife. I want a queen. And a queen makes sure of her own worth.

I could have her, and is she not worth a thousand Mistmere's?

"Do you promise to marry me if I surrender those territories to your mother?" The words are soft. Dangerous.

There's something about her expression that softens in disbelief.

"I promise. I promise once, I promise twice, I promise thrice. I will marry you if you give Mistmere to my mother."

Dark, silky lashes obscure my eyes as I try to hide the flare of possessive joy within me. She's mine. "Then I will hold you to your promise, Princess." I capture her hand, bringing it to my lips and brushing a soft kiss across the back of her knuckles. "Meet me at the Hammerdale ruins at midnight."

"And then?"

I can't help myself.

I kiss her.

Capturing her face between my hands I swoop down and claim that luscious mouth. A gasp escapes her, but then her fists are twining in my shirt. It doesn't matter if she's the daughter of my enemy. It doesn't matter if we barely know each other. We have this and it burns between us. A promise of more. A promise of forever if only I am brave enough to reach out and take it.

I draw back breathlessly, because I promised Eris I would be brief. "And then you belong to me. Forever."

10

ISKVIEN

Thiago did it.

He gave my mother Mistmere, simply gave those territories away as if they mean nothing to him. As if there hasn't been years of strife and bloodshed, two kingdoms holding a knife to each other's throat. As if Mistmere isn't the queen on the *fari* board that my mother and this prince have been playing to win for years, each determined not to yield.

He did it.

For *me*.

"What fucking game does he think he's playing?" my mother rages as she stalks circles around her tent. Her golden skirts rasp on the carpets that are laid everywhere, but the slither reminds me of nothing more than a serpent. "He'll *give* me Mistmere? And for what? For nothing? For *peace*."

"Maybe he's tired of war?" Edain murmurs, from where he's lounging on a daybed in the corner. He fingers a strand of grapes, his face blank and bored.

Andraste sits in the chair opposite him, casually stroking a cat. All her attention is focused on those long, gentle caresses, as if she doesn't dare even look at my mother.

I feel the tension too. Even from this little chair in the corner of the room. It's a surprise to find—after all these years apart—that there's something we still share.

We both recognize the warning signs.

Mother's fury starts small, and it builds like a storm on the horizon. Someone will suffer for this. Edain just pushed his way to the head of the list.

"Tired of war?" My mother turns on him like a snake about to strike. He's made himself a target by speaking up, but maybe he's spent too many years under her tender loving *care* to give a damn. "That bastard murdered the queen of Evernight, and then crushed any and all who opposed him. Thiago spent years wading through blood. He had the heads of Evernight's ruling princes mounted on the walls of his keep to show his city who ruled them now. And you think he's tired? Of war?"

Edain's sleepy-lashed look turns hot and insolent as he plucks a single grape from its strand. "Maybe the recent incapacitation of his friend, the hunter, has made him think twice about crossing you. They say he cares deeply for his circle of friends. He offered the borderlands for that bitch, Eris, after all, and there was nothing in it for him at the time. He didn't even know her. And I've never heard of anything that suggests he *actually* mounted his prince's heads on the battlements. Only the rumors."

Rumors. Which means she started them. I don't know why that thought makes it easier to breathe.

Maybe because I don't want to think Thiago the type of male who will guillotine someone and then stab their head onto a spike. That isn't the prince I know, who laid me on the grass and kissed his way down my body. That isn't the handsome stranger who looked at me with a smile in his eyes, as he captured my hand and lifted it to my lips.

"It doesn't make sense," my mother hisses. "No. There's some play here at hand." She presses her fingers to her temples. "I just can't see it. And if I can't see it then I don't know where he's going to strike from."

I can barely breathe.

The play is me.

I set the challenge before him.

Prove it. Prove I mean more to you than a chance to spite my mother. Prove your offer true.

The thought leaves me breathless and raw. I can't wait until tonight to see him. I can't wait to demand to know what he's thinking. It was a stupid challenge, thrown his way to stop this reckless foolishness. It was never meant to test his resolve. I didn't think he'd actually *do* it.

Because now it's my turn to roll the dice, and I don't know what to do.

Mother's right. There has to be some play here. Something long-term perhaps? Perhaps he cedes the southern half of Mistmere to my mother, marries me and—

And then what?

She's not going to grant him a dowry. She's not going to celebrate our marriage. If he gains something from this, then I can't see it, except for the horrible, breathless sensation that maybe it's me that he gains, but I'm worth nothing in the grand scheme of things and—

"Vi!" A set of fingers snaps right in front of my face and I freeze, because I lost focus on the true danger in the room, and now she's glaring down at me, leaning forward until both her hands are resting on the arms of the chair I sit in, caging me in. "Are you even listening to me?"

Mother's fingers dig into my chin, and my heart hammers in my chest because *fuck*, I've made myself a target by letting my thoughts drift.

"Of course I was listening." I have to salvage this moment, or I'm the one who will bleed for it. "I was just trying to think what he might gain by this."

"And?"

"Nothing." The word's soft. Dry. "He has nothing to gain. Unless…. Unless he seeks to make you out to be the aggressor. Perhaps this has something to do with the other queens and…." I almost say Kyrian's name, but she sees him as another male usurper. "Maybe it's got something to do with winning Queen Lucidia to his side. She votes for him as often as she votes against him, and with Queen Maren as your firm ally, and Pri… Kyrian as his, that leaves Lucidia to break any potential ties within the alliance." I'm babbling now, but she looks thoughtful. "Lucidia craves peace and if he offers the alliance peace, then she will ensure he remains in power to hold the balance."

She shoves away from me, and I almost fall out of the chair. "At least one of you is thinking." She taps her lip. "There was some rumor suggesting he and the eldest Ravenal princess sought to make a match." Her face darkens. "You're right. This goes further—deeper—than I could have suspected. We have to stop this alliance before he can wield it against me."

Punishment averted. I release a slow breath, but Edain is watching me from across the room with those implacable eyes. Sometimes I wonder if he sees far more than he ever reveals.

"How do we stop it?" Edain muses, tossing another grape in the air.

"You could kill the girl," Mother muses. "If I sent you to steal a knife from his tents, you could use that. Lay the blame at his feet."

Edain actually fumbles the grape, catching it before it hits the ground.

Andraste and I share a look.

It's rare that my mother makes a slip like that in front of us.

Edain stares at her flatly. "You want me to kill Lucere? With Thiago's knife?"

There's a certain sort of glee darkening her blue eyes. "Why did I not think of this before?" she breathes. "It's perfect."

"It's madness," Edain counters. He pushes himself upright, tossing the grapes aside as he locks gazes with her. "Firstly, I would have to be able to even get close to the Prince of Evernight. His people are—"

"Not that good." She whirls on him, and I can see her mind is made up. "Not as good as you when you want to be unseen."

"Firstly, if I *could* get close to him, then he would already be dead and we wouldn't be having this conversation," he points out, and I wonder if he's actually tried

161

before. "Secondly, the laws of the queensmoot are sacrosanct. No murder. No bloodshed. Any disputes must be brought before the alliance and the Council of Queens. If I am caught—fuck, if I actually kill the girl—then this doesn't just threaten the alliance, it shatters it. There will never be another queensmoot again." He holds up a finger when she moves to protest. "No, Adaia."

My mother leans forward, resting both hands on the daybed as she stares into his face. "What did you just say?"

"No," he repeats, loudly and firmly.

I don't dare move. I don't even dare breathe. Nobody tells her no, but Edain.... The way he's looking at her....

"Get out," she whispers, not bothering to look at us. "Both of you. I can see my little pet needs some convincing."

Edain's eyes smolder. He hates that nickname.

Andraste and I share a look.

I don't hesitate. I bolt for the tent opening.

Someone is going to die.

And the choices are: Lucere. Or Edain.

I HAVE TO SEE THIAGO AND I HAVE TO SEE HIM NOW.

It's no longer a matter of demanding to know what he meant by the Mistmere play—it's no longer important. Etan's the threat looming at my throat. And then there's Lucere, a princess with no idea what is even coming her way.

Mother will convince Edain to take a tilt at her. I'm

certain of it. The Queen of Asturia doesn't know what "no" means.

I have to stop this.

I have to stop Edain from getting close to Thiago and seeing war blow up in our faces.

And I owe Thiago a promise. I gave him my word that I would marry him if he gave my mother Mistmere.

It's all coming at me with the speed of a runaway carriage and I stuff my things into a bag, before grabbing my cloak and turning toward the door of the tent.

Too late. Andraste stands there, her gaze raking over the cloak, the knife and my dress. She draws her own conclusions. "Where are you going?"

"This is the last night of the queensmoot. I thought we were supposed to celebrate?"

She captures my wrist, searching my face. "Vi?"

"What if I told you there was a way I could… escape Etan?" I don't even know why I'm confiding in her, except for the fact that she's been kinder to me these past three days than she's been in years.

"I would say that you're a fool," she says gently. "Mother will never let you break the marriage contract."

"I have to believe, Andi. I have to have hope."

Andraste sighs. "Go," she whispers, holding the tent flap open. "Enjoy one last night of freedom."

I stare at her incredulously.

She shrugs. "I know you're not going to dance, Vi. You're going to go find your handsome stranger and you're going to spend the night in his arms. One of us may as well enjoy ourselves."

She thinks it's the last chance I have to enjoy another's

pleasures. I can see it in her face.

"I'm not going to stop fighting her," I tell her.

"I know." She grimaces. "You never do."

And then she pauses. "Do you remember the night you set fire to the castle?"

I wince as I draw my hood over my face. "I keep trying to forget it. I can barely look at a candle without flinching."

"It wasn't a candle, Vi." She says it so softly I can barely hear the words.

But a strange stillness seeps through me.

It feels like something inside me is holding its breath.

"She locked your magic away from you, made you forget it." Andraste fixes the hood of my cloak, even as her gentle words destroy me. Our eyes meet. "She's afraid of you. She's afraid of what you could achieve if you were ever to come into your power. You were nearly twelve and you burned half the castle down, Vi. I couldn't do that. Mother.... Mother could barely even quash the flames and her magic is strong. The only thing that stopped you was Nanny. Even broken and bleeding, she reached for your hand and she begged you to stop before you burned all of us alive."

The heat drains from my face.

I have magic.

Strong magic.

But no.... I can barely even light a candle. I can barely....

A single memory hammers itself through my brain: Screaming, heat, fire, a gnarled old hand squeezing mine as Nanny spat blood around a mangled, "Stop."

I flinch away from Andraste, clutching my head. It hurts.

It's like an ice prick to the brain.

"I... I remember." I can barely breathe.

My magic has always been weak and intractable, and my mother's made no secret of the fact she despises me for it.

But what does this mean?

Because if she took those memories away from me, if she took my magic, then why delight in sneering at me for it?

"Mother is going to name me heir once we return from the queensmoot," Andraste finally says. "Because she's afraid of you. She's afraid of what you could do if you ever come into your own. She mocks you and she locks you away, and she makes you believe you're weak. It's the same reason she's shipping you off to Aska."

"But I.... You...."

"I don't know if you *can* break the marriage contract," she says, "but don't you ever forget that you don't have to be afraid of Etan. He should be afraid of *you*. Enjoy this one last night, Vi, but don't be afraid of the future. If you're in Aska, then you have a chance to learn your magic without her watching over your shoulder. Learn it. Burn that fucking little creep alive if you need to. Become friends with Maren—she'd love a chance to help tear Mother down. Start playing your own game, start making the moves. You don't have to be the pawn anymore, Vi."

And then she holds the tent flap open.

I stare at freedom, my heart beating with the sound of Andraste's confessions.

With fury.

I promised the Prince of Evernight I would marry him, but it wasn't until this moment that I realize I *want* to marry him. I want to be free of my mother's machinations. I want to explore what it feels like to have a chance to fall in love with someone who believes in me. I want to know what kindness means, and what it feels like to fall asleep in the arms of a prince who will protect me from my mother's wrath.

I want to know if the way my heart skips a beat when he's around means something.

But what she says lights a fire in my heart.

Magic. Power. Strength.

I could have it all.

Andraste wants me to play the game? It feels like she's silently telling me to go ahead with my reckless plans.

Suddenly, all of my doubts about marrying the prince disappear.

"Thank you." I pause to kiss her cheek. "Thank you for telling me the truth."

Andraste won't meet my eyes. "I should have told you a long time ago. Now go…. Go and enjoy your last night of freedom before Mother realizes you're gone."

It's not my last night of freedom.

It's only the first.

And while I can't say goodbye to her, I have to say something. "You will make a fair and kind ruler of Asturia one day. You will be the kind of queen Mother could only dream of being."

And then I slip from the tent before she can even respond.

11

THIAGO

The moon hangs heavy in the skies over the Hammerdale ruins as we wait.

They're long broken—the remnants of a forgotten kingdom—and all that is left of them are fallen stone and jagged arches. The only thing that stands in any semblance of good quality is the temple, where an unknown goddess —or warrior—stares over the valley with a spear in her hand. The sculpted scallops of her gown are some of the finest work I've ever seen and the sight of her wings— each feather lovingly excavated from the alabaster marble —make my breath catch in my chest.

It also makes me wonder.

The fae of the Seelie alliance are purebred and can list their ancestors all the way back to the Great Exodus, when we fled the home world and colonized Arcaedia.

Wings don't belong on the fae.

Or not the Seelie.

No, the only winged fae they belong to lie in Unseelie.

I close my eyes and let my glamor shift over my skin. I

can feel the muscles stirring in my back as my wings slip into being. It's almost akin to shapeshifting. When I want to be Seelie, I swallow my Darkness whole. Wings, claws, those wretched soulless eyes that stare right through me in the mirror.

But they're always there.

Pressing beneath my skin. Threatening to consume me. One slip of my glamor and my true form rises to the surface.

I haven't told Vi the truth—there's so much I haven't told her—but what will she say when she sees my true form? The handsome prince with his green eyes and wicked smile is just a façade. It's a lie. A shield.

I want to be that prince with every part of my being, but the truth of my birth can't be denied.

I'm a monster trapped into fae flesh, and no matter how much I want to hide it, I can never forget.

Maybe you can finally submerge it once and for all if she marries you. Maybe she can help you vanquish this beast. You know how she makes you feel.

There's an incredible lightness in my chest when Vi smiles at me.

I'm no longer trapped in the dark, fighting not to drown.

No, I'm whole and handsome and able to lock my Darkness down so deep I could almost throw away the key. She's my hope and my salvation in one.

Marrying her means I finally get a good hand of cards. I'm no longer being tortured on Fate's rack. There is only goodness within Vi's heart. She can anchor me to this world, and I will give her everything.

My kingdom. My crown. My heart.

Gods, maybe even my heart.

If she cannot love me, *then can she ever truly love you?* whispers the Darkness within.

Be silent, I tell it.

What are you going to do? It taunts. *Are you going to lock me away and pretend I don't exist? Are you even going to tell her about me?*

I steel myself. *I don't know how she'll react. I just need time. Time to make her fall in love with me.*

Maybe if she loves me, then she will forgive me this one lie.

If I can just hold myself together long enough for Vi to want to stay with me....

The Darkness laughs. *I'll let you have this moment. Only because when I finally rise again, I'm going to enjoy your pain.*

But it sinks down deep inside me, until I can finally breathe again.

Will she come?

"Stop pacing," Thalia says, hauling me into place in front of her and brushing nonexistent lint of my doublet.

"I can't help it. Is there any sign of Baylor?"

I sent him to ensure Vi arrives safely at the ruins.

"She'll come," Thalia says, and I shake her free and rub my knuckles into the palm of my other hand as I pace.

Wanting someone as badly as I want Vi is like handing Adaia the knife and then not expecting her to put it to my throat.

What if this is the first mistake I make? What if I just took the wrong fork down a dangerous road?

I'm not a prince who is ruled by his impulses. I can't afford to give into anger or fear. The only way to cage the monstrosity within me is to chain every hint of emotion that flutters in my chest and control it.

But the truth remains.... I've had over six hundred years to master myself and the second I caught a glimpse of Vi, that control was shredded.

I want her.

Not just the woman who dragged my face down to hers for a kiss, or the woman who cried out in pleasure beneath me, but the one who demanded that I prove myself true— her dark eyes flashing with heat and fire. The one who crept into my tents with Finn slung over her shoulder, care- less of the blood that dripped down her fine gown or the fact she was in an enemy quadrant.

Vi understands what it's like to live one's life in a cage, and yet there's a kindness and generosity that has managed to survive everything her mother threw at her. Maybe, if her mother had her for another hundred years, she'd manage to strip Vi of her innocence, but I can't help thinking that she'd never manage to ruin her heart. There's defiance there. Stubbornness. And determination.

Vi wants to escape, just as much as I want to rescue her.

I asked Maia for a queen that long-ago night, but in my heart of hearts I begged her for the love of my life. Vi could be both. She's young, untried, her heart still fragile and uncertainty tearing at her every move, but I've seen the fire. I know it's there. I know—that with a little careful guidance—she will blossom into a woman who is a force to behold.

She just needs someone who will believe in her.

She just needs to take this step.

To come to me.

Will she come?

"I hope you know what you're doing," Eris murmurs at my side.

I lock it all down. "I know what I'm doing."

"Because this means war if you're wrong." Her gaze meets mine head-on. It's what I've always admired about her. She's never afraid to voice her doubts, never afraid to hesitate when it comes to protecting our kingdom—our people. Eris will give her all, no matter what choice I might make. Even if it means standing against me. "And I'm not talking about the border skirmishes and games we've been playing with Asturia to this point. I'm talking about brutal battles. I'm talking about winner takes all, Thiago."

"Then we will win," I assure her. "You and Baylor are the best we have. You're the reason that Adaia hasn't dared launch a full-scale offensive."

There's something in her eyes that makes my breath catch. Eris looks away. "You don't play the games Adaia plays. I don't play those games. And Baylor certainly doesn't. When I say war, I don't expect to be fighting in the trenches, Thiago. The knife will come from a direction we don't expect."

I can't deny it. "Maybe this will bring about peace. A true peace."

Neither of us believe it.

"I don't understand this. You don't make decisions like this. You don't let your heart rule your head. You're not thinking clearly. She's pretty, Thiago, I'll give you that, but you barely know her."

"I know enough," I counter. "She returned Finn to us, despite the fact her mother would punish her if she knew it was her hand that opened that cage. She is brave and honest and kind."

"She's the—"

"She's my promise." The words snap between us, landing like a blow. "Eris." I try to breathe through the knot in my chest. "She's my salvation. I *have* to believe that. And you alone…. You have to know what that means to me."

A sudden movement cuts through the tension. A hooded figure appears, right on the edge of the mists.

Vi.

Suddenly none of it matters. She lifts her hands to the hood of the cloak and then lowers it. Our eyes meet, and suddenly none of it matters.

She came.

She came alone.

Baylor stalks out of the shadows and she throws him a surprised look as if she wasn't even aware of him.

But then my gruff warlord does something totally unexpected. He offers his arm to her. "Allow me to walk you to my prince."

That he would offer this means everything to me.

I don't just want Vi to be my wife, I want my friends to welcome her.

They walk together, and I can see her breath catching, see hope and doubt warring within her. She's beautiful. As beautiful as a moon-kissed night. Indeed, she was made for night, with those gorgeous, wide eyes and the tumble of dark hair spilling down her back. She wears her starlight dress again, and as she walks toward me, the cloak slips from her shoulders, leaving them bare.

"Hello, Princess."

She glances up at me shyly as Baylor offers me her hand. "Hello, my husband."

There's a thickness in my throat as she takes my hands.

All my life I've lived for this. I've seen her face in every moment. I've pictured her so many times I could have almost conjured her from my dreams. When the world felt heavy on my shoulders, when the Darkness within threatened to choke me, I would reach out and bring her to life in my mind. She would turn and smile at me— the same way she did in the image Maia granted me—and hope would blaze to life in my heart. No matter what odds were stacked against me, no matter how much my shadows whispered to me, she was out there. Somewhere. In some time. Waiting for me.

And I just had to hold on until I could find her.

And now she's here and she's mine, and yet everything I thought I knew about her is wrong.

She's shorter than I'd ever imagined.

More watchful and older than her years. Those dark eyes drink in everything around her, as if she's siphoning the mood of the room before she dares speak. Reckless in some ways, yes. Or she wouldn't be marrying me. But there's a tension to her mouthiness, as if she's waiting for the consequences. Bold and brave enough to dare speak her mind, but prepared for pain. Expecting it. Anticipating it.

And the brash words hide her inner heart.

You don't get a piece of me, says the twitch of her brow.

You don't get that combination without some sort of abuse.

She'll protect others, but she thinks she stands alone. And her defiance is still skin deep. It consists of careless words, a breathless shrug and then those fists clenching as she prepares to endure. Convincing her to take this step with me was the hardest battle, because I'm asking her to fight back. I'm asking her to truly defy her mother. Not with words, not by locking her heart away where it can't get hurt, but by risking everything.

Discovering the truth of her birthright was a shock, a punch to the face. It hurt, because it smashed my dreams to pieces. All I could see was Adaia.

I didn't even think of what it would be like to be raised by that snake.

I barely know her.

But I know this: Hope.

"Are you ready?" I ask.

Vi lets out a shudder. "I'll never regret this." She lifts those midnight blue eyes to mine. "I want you to know that. This is the first choice I've ever made for myself. I will *never* regret it."

It's a knife to the chest.

The Darkness chuckles within me.

"Good." I don't know how I manage the word, but it's clearly less than she expected, and I can't explain....

"Do you, Thiago of Evernight, pledge your troth to the Princess of Asturia?" The priestess binds our hands together with a silken cord. It will stay bound until dawn breaks the sky. "In the name of Maia, in the name of the blessed light, do you promise to pledge your heart and soul to this woman?"

"I promise." There's no more doubt within me.

"Will you grant her forever by your side?

"I promise."

"Will you shield her from darkness and allow only light into your heart?"

It's harder to make this pledge, because the darkness is within *me*. But I'll protect her from that. I won't let them hurt her. I won't ever give into the monster inside me, the one that hungers and yearns. I will be everything she needs me to be. And *that* is what I can promise.

"I promise." Capturing Vi's face with my free hand, I lean down and whisper against her lips. "You are my light in the darkness. You are everything I've ever yearned for. I will love you forever, if only you let me. I promise now. I promise thrice. Thus let it be said, thus let my oath stand unbroken."

"*I promise now. I promise thrice. Thus let it be said, thus let my oath stand unbroken,*" whispers the Darkness.

There's a shiver of heaviness in the air, a sense of something listening. It feels like there's a storm on the horizon, the air thick with tension, but there's no sign of any clouds on the horizon.

Even the priestess looks up from her book.

Maybe it's the Hallow? There is power in these old places, after all. Or maybe... the Darkness spoke those words into the world and something heard them.

The thought rouses a shudder. *Be gone.*

Vi glances around as if she feels it more than me.

But I brush my lips against hers, and her distraction is shattered. She leans into me, kissing me back so softly it makes my heart sing.

I've won.

I've finally found her.

I'm never letting her go. Never.

The priestess turns to her. "Do you, Iskvien of Asturia, pledge your troth to the Prince of Evernight? In the name of Maia, in the name of the blessed light, do you promise to pledge your heart and soul to this male?"

"I promise." Iskvien whispers, and then she promises twice more.

"Now, you're mine," I whisper. "And nobody can ever take you away from me. Ever."

This time, I take my time in kissing her.

Because now, we have forever.

12

ISKVIEN

Hours later, we lie entwined in each other's arms. I can still feel Thiago inside me, and his kisses mark my skin, but there's something to be said for this moment. It was always easier to pretend this was nothing more than lust, and yet it's these moments that steal into my heart and threaten it.

He says he feels the same way, but....

Everything has happened so fast.

It's not love. It can't be love. Can love even be forged in a mere three days?

But it's something.

I just don't know what to name it, precisely.

"What are you thinking about?" he murmurs, kissing my shoulder from behind.

"Nothing."

A pair of fingers grip my chin and then he's turning my face toward him in order to meet my eyes. "Oh no, Vi. None of that here. Not between us anymore. Only the truth now."

Rebellion brews in my heart. The only way I've survived these past eight years is by locking my heart away and not daring to give voice to the parts of me that matter.

I did that once.

I loved. I begged for love in return. I *was* loved.

And that door was slammed shut in my face as though it never existed.

"Talk to me." It's not a demand.

"We barely know each other." I can't help feeling the weight of that choking me. "Everything's happened so fast."

"Precisely my point. Talk to me." Thiago shifts a little, until my head is resting on his chest. It's difficult to manage with our wrists still bound together, but he's patient. "Let me know you. This doesn't work if we can't learn how to share ourselves."

Share ourselves.... My hand stills over his heart. I don't even know if I can do that.

"Why me?" I finally put a voice to the feelings inside me.

"Why not you?"

"Because I'm the enemy," I point out in exasperation. Put like that, none of this makes sense. "Because you took one look at me and you decided then and there that you wanted me—"

"We discussed this."

I don't know where they come from, but the words just tear loose. "And maybe you weren't convincing enough."

The second they're out, I want them back.

But Thiago merely props one hand under the back of

his neck, so his face tilts enough that he can see me. He sighs. "Do you want to hear a story?"

"Only if it has some means of explaining this."

"It does—only you don't believe in fate."

I eye him dubiously. "I thought that was only a line you used to seduce me."

He shakes his head. "I never lie, Vi."

"Then tell me your story."

"Five hundred years ago, I was in… a bad place. I had done something so foolish that I could never take it back again, and I knew that come morning, I would have to face my daemons."

"What did you do that was so bad?"

Our eyes meet.

And rage smolders to life in his eyes. "I intended to kill my father. I worked my way into a position where I would be able to murder him. I thought I was finally strong enough to do so, and I was waiting for him in an ambush, the knife in my hand… when I finally laid eyes on him." He brushes his fingers against my thigh. "I knew in an instant I had made a mistake. My father is a monster. He was centuries older than me at the stage. Warped by Darkness. Twisted. And I hesitated just long enough that he passed my ambush and all I could do was sit in the snow and shake.

"I returned to the nearest city, furious with myself for wasting my chance. Even if I couldn't kill him, I needed to confront him. I yearned for it so badly I barely ate. Barely slept. My friend, Cian, tried to talk sense into me but I was lost to his words." He shudders. "Cian told me I was becoming exactly what I hated so much. I was slowly

179

losing myself to the same Darkness. If I didn't give up this course then it would consume me." Thiago's eyes darken. "I hit him. I didn't want to listen. I hit him until he stopped talking and then I walked into those streets blindly. I was no longer in control of myself. I was exactly what he said I'd become. I was my father. And when I looked into the nearest shop window, all I could see was that bastard staring back at me from the reflection."

I can barely breathe as I trace small circles on his chest. "What happened?"

"It frightened me so much I fled to the nearest temple of Maia. I was begging, desperate, on my knees in the middle of Her courtyard. Show me the light, I said. Give me a single sign this rage will end. Give me a shred of hope. Tell me I'm not a monster.

"Lightning flashed. And there you were." His lashes shield his eyes. "Staring back at me from the waters of the Pool of Serenity. You glanced back over your shoulder and smiled at me, and I knew you would be mine. One day. All I had to do was wait for you to come and find me. And every time I found myself lost in the Darkness, I would close my eyes and think of your face. Of your smile. And I would know hope."

He opens his eyes, seeing the shock in mine.

And he smiles.

"Of course I came for you the second I saw you dancing. How could I resist my salvation, Vi? How could I turn away from Fate? I was made for you, and you were made for me. I recognized you the moment I saw you."

I suck in a slow breath. Of all the things I ever expected, it was not a confession like this.

It places an incredible amount of pressure on me.

But it also feels tremulously like there's finally a place for me.

I will never be alone again.

Thiago kisses my forehead and draws me into his arms. "I just needed to wait until you were finally born."

"How did you find your way to Evernight?"

"Another story. A longer story." His voice roughens. "I wanted a home. I wanted... something for myself. Something nobody could ever take from me. And so I took it. I claimed the throne. I became the Prince of Evernight. And I crushed any and all who opposed me."

There's a long silence. I've heard it all before, of course—*bastard-born prince; traitor; ambitious, murderous male*—but I've never heard it from his own lips.

"I still want it all." There's a hunger in his voice. "I have the people who have become my family. I have a castle, a fucking kingdom, a throne. It's not enough. It was never enough. I want a wife. I want a family. I want to be *normal*—"

"Normal?" There's something about that one word that captures my attention.

He stills. It's a cool, controlled tension—so different from my mother's—as if he locks it all down inside him, and breathes it out through his lungs. "There's a darkness inside me, Vi. One I've fought against every day of my life." A tiny little shudder runs through him, almost imperceptible. If I wasn't pressed up against him like this, I would have missed it. He looks into my eyes and his thumb brushes against my lips. "I'd be lying if I said it didn't scare me. I'd be lying if I told you it was locked away inside me, guarded by walls so thick it will never escape." His voice roughens as his vision goes distant. "There are cracks in those walls. Sometimes the shadows slip through. Sometimes they whisper to me. I can feel it calling to me. I can feel the hunger, the yearning. It's me. It's the Darkness inside me. All I've ever wanted is to be whole, but if I do that, then maybe *I* cease to exist. Or the part of me that wants to hold you in my arms, to cling to you like you're my lifeline. The part of me that could love you."

My heart goes still. A lead weight in my chest. I don't know what to say.

I don't even truly know what he's talking about.

And he sees it.

Thiago shoves himself upright. "Maybe it was wrong of me not to tell you first. To give you a choice."

"You did give me a choice," I protest, sitting up and dragging the cloak to my breasts. "As I recall, I promised you forever. No matter what. I knew there are shadows within you. I knew I was taking a chance. I still made that choice. I'd still *make* that choice."

He looks at me then. "Even if you just married a monster?"

I look at him and I can't see it. All I can see are doors slamming shut. Shouts echoing through the hallways of Hawthorne castle. People's faces cringing as my mother pronounces her whims upon the court. Vines stabbing up through the flagstone floors and spearing straight through a foreign emissary's throat when he insults my mother.

And me.

Stealing refuge in the library because it's the safest place in the castle. The constant pressure in my chest when I'm at court. Worrying that I'm wearing the wrong thing, saying the wrong thing, ingratiating myself to the wrong people.

Never daring to make friends or smile at one of the servants, because my mother will use them to hurt me if she thinks I care about them.

My mother would never care if anyone was afraid of her. Fear is the pressure point you push to get your own way, according to her.

If there was darkness inside her, she would embrace it. She would trample all in her path and laugh as people pleaded for mercy.

"I've seen monsters." It's a dawning realization I've never dared give voice. Here he is, worrying that the shadows inside him will take over. Worried that he hasn't given me a *choice* in this, because he hasn't given me all the information.

My mother has never once worried if her actions will be perceived the wrong way. It's always my fault when we argue, until I'm second-guessing every choice I make. It's always my actions, my choices, my lack of magic.... You spend your entire life trying to juggle plates, and it doesn't matter how well you juggle them, it feels like she's throwing more plates at you. Faster and faster, as if to try and force me to fail so she can punish me again.

She's a monster.

All those times I've apologized for something I haven't done. The guilt. The weight of it eating away inside me until I decided that maybe it would be just easier if I didn't care at all.

Maybe it would have been easier if she'd just *hit* me.

And that's a ticking time-bomb of a realization because I've never dared consider whether the hurt she's caused is… her fault. I've always allowed her to claim it as my own. I've always bowed my head and sought a way to make her happy—or if not happy, then to stop her from screaming. You try and you try and you try and it's never enough.

"She's hurt you." His hand strokes over my shoulder and down my back. Then up again, his thumb rasping over my cheek. It's a comforting thing. More than I ever expected really, and I shiver as I snuggle into his chest and wrap my arms around him.

"Yes." A quiet confession in the night.

It makes me feel as though I'm something precious and he can barely stop touching me. As if I'm going to vanish if he dares let me go, even for a second.

I want to hold onto this feeling forever.

"I *am* a bastard, Vi." It's a whisper in the night. "Because I knew what I was asking you to walk into blindly. And here you are, trying to flee a monster of your own making."

I slide a thigh over him, straddling his hips. "I'm not scared of you. I'm not scared of any part of you. Because if you were truly a monster then you wouldn't be warning me away."

He groans as he slides his hands up my sides. "Vi, Vi, you don't know what you're saying—"

I find his cock, hard beneath me and slick with my own

wetness. "If you give me the chance I will love every part of you. I promise you this. I will love your light. I will love your darkness. I will fight for you with everything I have." The tip of his cock breeches me and I shove down, sucking in a sharp breath as he fills me to the hilt. It's still new, still a shock to my body. And I love it. Love feeling those hands digging into my hips as he snarls and thrusts up into me. Together we can conquer the world.

"Show me your darkness," I whisper, threading our fingers together and riding him. "Let me love it."

A gasp escapes him and he throws his head back, his fingers clenching in mine. "You're too good to be true."

I lean down and nip at his throat. "No, I'm not. I'm tired of being good. I'm tired of being trapped in a cage, staring at the world through my own glass walls. Maybe I want to break free too. Maybe I want to be wicked. Maybe I want to *be* your queen." The words fill every inch of me, lighting me up within.

I've never had a dream. I've never dared.

But hearing his words, hearing the yearning in his voice…. I want that too. And maybe this was reckless, maybe it will bring ruin, but it feels like I'm setting fire to the old Vi and out of her ashes dawns a *new* version. A phoenix of resurrection that will forge me into something whole, something stronger, something that can take on the world and win.

I want to *be* this Vi.

He's given me that.

The chance to bloom.

I won't ever let him surrender to the weight that bears him down.

13

THIAGO

The final morning of the queensmoot dawns, and
with it, the last meeting of the alliance.

The Council of Queens makes its way toward the enormous rocky outcropping that looms over the field of tents.

"I hope you know what you're doing," Eris tells me.

So do I. "Enough, Eris. It's done."

She spent half the night prowling around the Ravenal
camp, ostensibly to protect Princess Lucere from any
threat Edain might offer.

Nothing ever eventuated, despite Vi's insistence that
her mother was going to try to kill the princess.

And Eris likes her sleep.

She looks like she wants to murder someone today.

I'm still wearing the braided strip of material around
my wrist that bound me to Vi for the night. When dawn
kissed the sky she slipped from my arms, pressing a finger
to my lips to still my protest before she kissed me.

"*I have to return,*" she whispered. "*Just this once. My
mother must never suspect what has happened until it's too*

186

late. We don't dare give her the opportunity to plan ahead."

We spent half the night plotting together about how to play this.

Adaia's fury is a storm. It builds and builds and builds, finally breaking over you and hammering you until you're bloody and defeated. We can't afford to have her fore-warned. Vi is leaving with me as soon as this meeting is done, before Adaia has time to launch a counterattack.

Eris chafes at the order, but she nods. "Fine. The tents are being stripped as we speak. Lysander's in charge. He thinks we should be packed and prepared to evacuate within the hour. Baylor's got ten warriors nearby, just in case. We didn't dare bring any more. We leave as soon as this is done."

I nod and duck beneath the lintel stones of the Hallow.

Adaia shoots me a glare from where she's murmuring something to Maren. Lucidia merely looks curious, as if wondering why I changed my mind about our negotiations yesterday.

Kyrian is late, as usual, taking his seat soon after I take mine.

I've barely seen him this queensmoot and the look he shoots me says he's aware of it.

Something I should know about, asks the quirk of his brow.

"Another chair, if you will?" I say to the attendant, loudly enough to snag the attention of my fellow rulers.

The attendant blinks. This is unheard of, and yet he snaps his fingers and a chair is produced, albeit somewhat less ornate than the one I—and the other rulers—sit in.

Four sets of eyes lock upon me.

"You need two chairs, Thiago?" Adaia's lip curls in disdain.

"Perhaps it's for his ego," Maren murmurs, smirking into the glass of water one of her servants has produced. She looks like she spent the night frolicking and is paying for her sins this morning.

Lucidia's eyes narrow. She alone seems to sense the tides shifting.

"Yesterday, when we met, I spoke of peace," I reply, lounging back in the thronelike chair. "I offered a conciliatory gesture toward the Queen of Asturia, and I am here to hammer out the details of such an arrangement."

"Mistmere is not yours to offer," Adaia hisses, no doubt smarting from the loss of her bargaining chip.

"But it is mine to concede," I counter.

"I thought you were no longer interested?" Lucidia asks.

"In peace? Yes. Though the terms have shifted."

Adaia visibly seethes.

Queen Maren taps her long red nails against her painted lips. "I cannot help but think such an offer seems too good to be true. Why would you *give* away any rights to Mistmere? This is not done out of the kindness of your heart so you must forgive us if we question your motives."

"What do you get out of this?" Lucidia asks bluntly.

"Peace. I speak of an alliance between two kingdoms that have been at each other's throats for far too long." I meet Lucidia's eyes and then Maren's. "The enmity between Evernight and Asturia affects us all. It weakens us against the threat of Unseelie."

"This alliance." Lucidia leans forward hungrily. "What would it consist of?"

"There have been treaties in the past," Kyrian adds. "All broken. Why should this one be any different?" He cuts a look toward Adaia. "She's not going to play by the rules."

"Because… this time there is a reason for both Evernight and Asturia to hold the peace." I stand and glance back to where Eris, Lysander and Finn stand guard, holding out my hand. "Vi?"

Finn and Lysander step aside and there she is, visibly swallowing. Gowned in white, she steels herself, tips her chin up and then strides forward with her skirts bunched in both hands. It's the look of a queen focusing on the guillotine ahead of her. Defiant and proud until the last, but also choking down the lump of fear in her throat.

"What is the meaning of this?" Adaia pushes to her feet abruptly. "Iskvien, what are you doing here?"

"She is here because I asked her to be here," I reply. "She is here because she is the answer to the war between our countries."

Vi takes my hand, her fingers warm in mine, and I give them a squeeze. *Look at me. Look at me and not at her.*

It's as if she hears me.

Our eyes meet and though she shields her emotions well, I can see she's merely waiting for the lash of the whip to fall.

"A marriage," I say softly, though my focus is on her. "A marriage between two countries in order to hold the peace. Evernight will yield any claim to the lands of Mistmere if the Queen of Asturia stands her armies down and allows this marriage."

"*Marriage*?" Etan of the Goldenhills shoves out of the Askan delegation, his face mottling with color. "But she is already promised! To me!"

Maren holds out a hand toward him, her cold eyes never shifting from my face. Etan—to his detriment—doesn't notice her warning, and takes another step forward. Muraid, Maren's lover and most dangerous general, shoves him back into place. He meets her gaze, but whatever he sees there makes him flinch.

He *should* cower.

Vi was hiding from him the first night we met, and while I haven't bothered to consider him a threat, I don't like the way he looks at her. There's something violent in that look, something threatening. Something possessive that doesn't speak of an intent to protect and love, but the instinct to smother.

Rip his fingers from their sockets, Ruin whispers, and he's usually the least violent of the creatures trapped within me.

"Control your dog," I tell Maren with quiet menace.

"How dare you speak to her like that?" Adaia's face goes red. "How dare you lay claim to *my* daughter? I don't care what you offer me, you'll never have her. *Never.* As Etan mentions, I have promised her hand to him and the contracts are already—"

"Her hand is not yours to give," I tell her coolly. "Vi is of age. It's her choice."

"Iskvien is *mine* and she signed those contracts of her

own free will. If you think I will ever grant you my blessing to marry her—"

"I'm not asking for permission, Adaia." I tug Vi onto the throne at my side. "It is done. Vi agreed to marry me last night and our union was blessed by a priestess of Maia."

You're too late.

"You what?" Adaia's eyes threaten to bulge out of her head. "You little slu—"

"That's enough." It takes everything I have not to slip into the shadows right now. "You will not speak to her like that again. She is a princess of Evernight now."

"You speak of peace and ruining alliances, but you have no idea what you've done." Adaia hisses. "Iskvien was betrothed to Etan of the Goldenhills, and her wedding was bound to cement an alliance between Aska and Asturia. It's not just me you think you've thwarted. Maren, tell him. She signed the contract!"

Queen Maren is Etan's aunt.

But she merely strokes her fingers along the edge of her carved chair, her glittering eyes watching the entire affair play out. Of all the queens in the alliance, she's the one I am most wary of. Maren plays the long game, and while she's not openly ambitious the way Adaia is, she's dangerous in a way the Asturian queen could never hope to match.

"Any wedding officiated by a priestess of Maia is legitimate," Maren murmurs slowly. Her attention focuses on Iskvien. "Unless the princess can claim she was coerced."

"No." Iskvien stares them all down, including her mother. "There was no coercion. I married him of my own free will." This time when she turns to her mother, there's a growing confidence within her. "I married him because I wanted to. I married him because I wanted peace between our two countries, peace for the alliance. And I married him because… because I think I could come to love him."

I never dared wish for such a thing. *Love*. It's only been three days, but the suggestion knots hard around my own heart.

Vi turns to Maren. "My apologies for the deception, Your Majesty, but if there was ever coercion involved, it was in forcing me to sign that contract. My mother threatened to kill someone if I did not do so. I never wished to deceive you."

"Enough of this nonsense," Adaia snaps. "Come here."

Like she's talking to a dog.

"No." Vi stares her down. "I have *made* my decision. We are *married* and the marriage is consummated. It is too late to deny it."

"You had no right." Adaia shakes with fury as she glares at me. "She is mine and you have stolen what is mine. There will be no peace. None. I will not—"

"You have no cause to deny the marriage," Maren cuts in. "It is done, Adaia. Done."

The two queens stare at each other.

"Then I will have recompense," Adaia snaps.

"You have the disputed territories in Mistmere," Lucidia points out. "What more could you wish?"

"My daughter." Adaia turns all her fury upon Vi. "He has stolen my *daughter*. He has turned her against me—"

"He never turned me against you," Vi bursts out, as if

she's unable to hold her frustration within her. "You did that yourself."

"See!" Adaia gestures toward her as she begs the other queens. "In three mere days my beloved child has gone from being content and happy in my arms, to being defiant and disobedient. You've all seen her before. You've all met her. She's changed! He's ensorcelled her."

"I've done nothing of the sort."

But Maren looks thoughtful and Lucidia reaches out to accept a glass of wine from the tray her granddaughter—Lucere—provides.

"It is not enough to offer me mere lands," Adaia seethes. "Is Mistmere meant to comfort me on those nights when my child is gone from my arms?"

"It didn't seem to bother you when you were selling me to Etan," Vi grinds out between her teeth.

I lace a hand over hers. "You grow greedy, Adaia. I would have thought you longed for peace."

Adaia's eyes glitter with malice.

Peace has never been an option between us. The only thing that will ever appease her will be my head on a stake.

"Prince Thiago speaks the truth," Kyrian murmurs, finally speaking up from where he lounges with insolent grace, swinging his crown around his finger. "The Alliance has long wished for peace between all our kingdoms. Perhaps this marriage will cement such a notion. Perhaps it is necessary."

"But Adaia also speaks truly," Maren murmurs, "Iskvien is her daughter. Is she to lose her daughter from her side forever? If Iskvien was to marry into my court then Adaia would be free to visit her, and Iskvien allowed to return to her mother's court for important gatherings. One marriage is not the same as the other. It seems cruel to lose a child you love so dearly."

Vi tenses as if she wishes to retort, but I squeeze her hand. "I would never deny my wife if she wished to return to her mother's court for such gatherings. It would be her choice."

When the Underworld turns to flames, says the stubborn jut of Vi's chin.

Kato's realm is as cold, barren and lifeless as the tundra in the far north.

Adaia sinks onto her throne. "Whether the marriage is consummated or not, you went behind my back to steal my daughter. You married her in secret. You stole her from me. And regardless of your fucking offer to allow her to return at whim, I find I care little for such assurances. You lie as well as you breathe, Evernight. So I will offer you a little bargain, if you dare…."

Don't trust her, whispers the Darkness within me.

For once it seems to be working in alignment with me.

I don't, I tell it.

"What do you have in mind?" I ask.

"I fear Iskvien has made a foolish bargain over the course of a mere three days," she replies. "I would hate for her to regret such impulsiveness. You may have her. For three months of the year, one for every day she has known you. As spring beckons you will return her to me for the rest of the year."

"Absolutely not."

She leans forward, a serpent about to strike. "You say you haven't ensorcelled her? Then prove it. Nine months at my side is long enough to break any enchantment, and we shall know the truth. If she chooses to return to you at the next queensmoot, then I will believe her heart is true."

"You say you don't trust me? Then the reverse is also true. If I give her back to you, then I fear I will never see her again," I counter.

"I will swear such a thing before the alliance," Adaia replies coldly.

There has to be some trick to it. But I can't see it. "You will not use your magic to deny her the ability to say she loves me. You will not turn her heart to ice. You will not kill her, or harm her, or allow anyone else to do so either."

Adaia curls her lip. "I don't need to, little princeling. She barely knows you. Once she realizes what kind of monster she's tied herself to, then she'll come crawling back to me."

I don't know why cold panic grips me. "One year is not enough."

The smile that spreads across her face shows no mercy. "Your doubt reveals your intentions—"

"As I said, I don't trust you at all. Fifty years."

"Three."

"Forty."

"Four."

At my side I sense Vi tensing.

"Thirty-five."

"Five."

"That's enough," Vi gasps. "Enough! Do I not have any say in this?"

"Forgive me." I've been alone for so long that making such decisions by myself is instinct.

Or maybe it's just instinct to start firing back the second Adaia opens her mouth.

But if I keep doing that, then Vi is going to be the one caught in the middle.

"Thirteen," says Lucidia, her voice cracking through the tension like a whip.

"*What*?" For once, both Adaia and I echo each other.

"An auspicious number," Lucidia continues. "You will have thirteen years to win her heart, Prince Thiago. Every winter, you will have her for your own. Every spring, you will return her to her mother for nine months." Those gimlet eyes turn to Adaia. "And likewise. The disputed territories in Mistmere will be held in trust by the alliance. By the time the thirteenth queensmoot arrives, the princess must make her final choice. She must choose to stay with her mother, or to fully accept her role as the Prince of Evernight's wife. Whoever wins will take both the girl and the territories."

"That is not what he said yesterday," Adaia spits, on her feet once again and furious. "He *gave* them to me."

"And you said they weren't enough," Lucidia counters, "not when it came to your daughter's heart, though I find it interesting you didn't bother to mention Iskvien, just now. Is that what you want, Adaia? He's offered you Mistmere in exchange for her hand. Just say the word, and those lands are yours."

Fury blights those almond-shaped green eyes. Our stares meet, and my thumb, casually stroking Vi's hand, goes still.

Say it. Agree to it.

Take the fucking lands.

But perhaps she sees my eagerness.

"Thirteen years then," Adaia whispers. "Thirteen years before Iskvien must make her final choice. But if you lose, then I will take your life too. For the audacity in daring to touch my daughter."

"I'm not going to lose." I have to trust in fate. I have to trust in Vi.

"Then swear it," she hisses. "Swear it thrice, or I am done with this entire mockery of a treaty. Or do you not trust her love?"

"I swear it," I snap. "I swear it once, twice, thrice."

Vi gasps. "No!"

I squeeze her hand. "I trust you. I trust what we have. You will never choose her. I know that."

She swallows. "It's not me that I don't trust."

I lift her hand to my lips and kiss it. It doesn't matter what Adaia does; she can't destroy the promise of what we have.

"So be it." Adaia draws herself to her full height, smiling darkly. "Enjoy the next three months, my darling daughter. I shall see you again come the spring."

And then she turns and stalks from the Hallow, taking all of the oxygen with her.

"What in the Underworld were you thinking?" Thalia demands, the second we're safely in my council chambers inside the castle of Ceres.

She hasn't dared raise her voice before then.

Too many ears who didn't need to hear this argument.

197

"I was thinking that I would have her despite the costs," I snap. "Adaia wasn't going to back down."

"You offered your *life*," Thalia growls out. "You played directly into that bitch's hands."

It's Vi who comes to the rescue.

"His life is safe," she says into the ringing echo within the chamber. "I will never choose my mother. I swear it."

"She'll try to turn you against me," I warn. "She has nine months every year to do so."

Vi's smile is tremulous. "She can try. She's spent my entire life trying to mold me to her whims." A stubborn expression comes into her eyes. One that promises trouble for me, if I ever try to stand against her. "She didn't succeed then and she won't succeed now." She takes my hands in hers. "Thank you. You don't understand what it means to have someone fight for me like that."

"Always." I capture her mouth in a swift kiss.

We're home. We're safe.

I want to show her my world. I want to take her into my city and let her explore. But first, I want to pick her up, throw her over my shoulder and carry her off to our chambers.

Someone clears a throat.

"As lovely as it is to see you so happy," Finn says, "it's starting to get a little awkward for the rest of us."

I make a rude gesture in his general direction and then finally break the kiss. "Get used to it. Nothing is going to change—"

"For the next three months," Eris says.

She's sharpening a knife in the corner, her entire focus locked upon the blade.

As silence reigns, she looks up. "What?"

Sometimes I wish she didn't have to be so fucking honest.

"Then we have three months." Vi bites her lip and then offers me a shy smile. "I don't want to waste another moment on worrying about my mother. I want to see your city. I want to meet your people. I want to... be your wife."

There's a blush to her cheeks at those last words.

Gods, even now she sees the good in the moment. I squeeze her hand.

"Thalia, you're in charge of my city," I tell her, making a sudden decision.

"I am?" My cousin's eyebrows shoot up.

"You are." I take a backwards step toward the door. "Don't burn it down. Don't blow it up. And don't let your demi-fey take over the keep. Finn, you're in charge of helping Eris get that stick out of her ass."

"Me?" Finn holds his hands out. "Why are you throwing *me* to the wolves?"

Eris gives me a long, slow, unamused look.

"Where are *you* going?" Lysander looks intrigued.

"My wife and I are going to take a honeymoon," I tell them all. "I want to forget about murderous queens and broken alliances. I don't want to even hear a single murmur about politics. I am taking Vi to Valerian, where the only thing that might bother us is the wraiths."

"You're going to freeze your ass off," Baylor mutters.

Vi clears her throat. "I don't have very much magic, but if there's one thing I am good at, it's setting things on fire."

I wink at him. "There. You see. Toasty warm." I give her a considering look. "You set things on fire?"

"Long story." Vi's face closes over. "Maybe I'll tell you about it when those nights are cold."

"I'm fairly certain no stories will get a chance to be told," Thalia says, as she shoos us toward the door. "Go. Have fun. Don't do anything I wouldn't do."

"Well, that limits the options," Baylor says.

"Ha, ha, you're so amusing." She scrunches up a piece of paper and throws it at him. "Don't make me put you on guard duty for the next fortnight. You heard him. I'm in charge."

"Maia save our souls," Lysander says mournfully, looking toward the sky as if he's praying directly to the goddess.

There's a shy smile on Vi's face as she takes them all in.

This. This is what I wanted to show her. This is what I want her to be a part of.

But in the meantime....

"Are you coming?" I ask, offering her my hand.

"Maybe soon," she whispers, with a teasing twinkle in her eye as she accepts my hand.

We haven't been alone since I won the right to have her.

"Definitely soon," I promise, as I draw her through the door and kiss her in the hallway outside.

EPILOGUE

 *ne year later....*

It's been eight months, twenty-nine days and seventeen hours since I last saw my wife.

I feel every single one of those days as I stand in the Hallow at Hammerdale and wait for Adaia to arrive with my wife.

"She's coming," Thalia murmurs, laying a sympathetic hand on my arm. "Stop pacing. Maren is watching."

"It's nearly evening." They should have been here by now. I can't help thinking that Adaia has one last trick up her sleeve, and this delay only tightens my nerves.

The last time I saw Vi she told me she loved me.

Those words were hard-won by months of sweet kisses and quiet conversations, but also by the growing feelings within me. I've always carried her in my heart as a sign of hope, but I never realized that having her would be more than mere fate. I fell in love with her over those months, and in the end, I was the one who said it first.

They were the very last words she spoke to me.

"Relax, Your Highness," Lucidia says, laughing under her breath. "You will have your wife by your side soon enough. Adaia cannot thwart the entire alliance."

Maren says nothing.

That only makes me feel more uncomfortable.

The Hallow starts to pulse with light. Bells ring as the servants who rope off the Hallow cry the bells in order to alert anyone within the vicinity—the portals can be dangerous magic. Fae who have been caught within the stones when someone ignites the portals have disappeared in the past.

"Here they come," Finn says, clapping a hand on my shoulder.

Light blazes and a shadowy party appears in the center of the Hallow. The bannerman comes first, the red pennant of Asturia snapping straight in the wind, revealing those mocking roses and the crown of thorns. Servants pour through the stones. And then the lords and ladies of Asturia, and finally, finally, the queen and her royal family.

Edain stalks out first, one hand resting on the hilt of his sword as the Asturian guards spread out. There's something in his eyes as our stares meet—I don't know what to name it. Pity, perhaps. Or maybe disdain. He's hard to read.

The crown princess alights at his side, but I barely bother to give her a glance.

Because Vi is there.

One hand tucked in her mother's arm as if she's old

and infirm.... Or no, it looks almost like Adaia has one hand shackled around her wrist.

"Vi." I can't take my eyes off her, letting my gaze run hungrily over her.

I can't see any sign of bruising, but there's no smile on her face. Only dark circles beneath her eyes, and the same starburst gown she wore the first time we met.

I start toward her, but Eris plants a hand in the center of my chest. "Wait."

"I've waited long enough."

"Then look at her," my general snaps. "There's something wrong. That doesn't look like Vi anymore. Adaia's done something to her."

My heart starts to sink like a lead weight. *No*. Adaia promised she wouldn't harm her. She swore she wouldn't threaten her or punish her in any way....

"Vi." I push past Eris's restraining grip, intent on only one thing: taking my wife in my arms and ensuring Adaia hasn't hurt her.

"Mother." Vi's face pales and she curls her fingers into her fist as she turns to her mother imploringly. "*Please. Please don't do this*—"

"That's enough." Adaia jerks her arm out of Vi's reach, her lip curling. "You will do your country proud. You will sacrifice yourself as tribute to keep the peace." Her smile turns sinister. "That's what you want, isn't it? Peace?"

The words are a blow.

I slam to a halt, barely feet away from my wife.

But she's not looking at me the way she always has.

Vi's shoulders straighten and she clearly forces herself

to meet my stare, but nothing has changed. She looks as if she's steeling herself.

She looks at me as if I'm a monster.

What in the Underworld has Adaia done to her?

"Yes," she whispers, and swallows hard. "I... I want peace."

"Vi?" I don't understand. There's no spell that could have hardened her heart against me. Adaia swore she wouldn't turn her heart to ice. She swore.

Drawing her hood over her dark hair Iskvien glides toward me like a queen walking toward her doom. It's what I've been dreaming of all these months, and yet the tension in my gut knots tight.

This isn't a dream.

This isn't my wife, the woman I fell in love with.

This is... some sort of nightmare, conjured out of Adaia's cruelty and malice.

"Vi, you're finally here." I capture her cold hands. "You're—"

Vi wrenches her fingers from mine. "Get your hands off me, you monster. I may be forced into this little bargain between you and my mother, but that doesn't mean I won't fight you at every moment."

Monster.

This cannot be happening. The world reels around me.

"What did you do to her?" I demand of Adaia.

"A little wedding gift, Your Highness." Adaia smirks. "I was remiss in providing one last time."

"You swore you would not—"

"Hurt her, kill her, turn her heart to ice, or deny her the ability to tell you she loves you," Adaia says with a sneer.

"And I haven't. Perhaps she has finally opened her eyes to the truth?"

"Mother." Vi looks between us. She shakes her head as if she can hear something we can't. "What is going on?"

"You are to be given as tribute to the Prince of Evernight for three months in order to uphold a treaty," Adaia says. "As always, Asturia honors its word."

You fucking bitch.

"Vi." I reach for her again. "Vi, come here. What has she done to you? What's wrong? Tell me and I'll fix it."

"Don't touch me!"

"Vi, you're my wife. We were married at last year's Queensmoot. You're my wife. I love you."

"Your wife?" Her eyes go wide. But it's the sudden surge of lightning I see in her dark irises that makes my breath catch. Magic breaking. I swear I've seen something like that before…. In Unseelie.

"Vi?"

She moans and staggers to the side, pressing her fingers to her temple. "Stop it. I don't want to do this. Mother." She digs her nails into her hair. "Mother, make it stop. It's hurting. It's hurting. Please don't make me do this."

"What's hurting?" I try to touch her again, but she lashes out, staggering back.

And then her eyes roll back in her head—

I catch her as she falls, cradling her against my chest. Blood drips from her nose and she groans, her eyes fluttering as they roll up in her head.

"Thalia!"

Thalia captures Vi's face in her hands, her thumbs

caressing her cheeks. She has some small abilities with healing. She bites her lip. "Call for the medic! Her brain is bleeding, I think."

Bleeding— I shoot her a horrified look.

"It's bad," Thalia whispers, reading my mind. "A thousand tiny little bleeds as if something tore through her mind."

I seek and find Adaia's merciless gaze and my words come out hoarsely. "What did you do to her?"

The queen smiles malevolently. "Me? *I* did nothing. This is all your doing, you wretched prick. You think you can steal from me and remain unpunished—?"

"I stole *nothing* that wasn't given freely." Hot fury leeches through my brain. Vi looked at me as if I was a stranger, a monster. She didn't recognize me.

And now there's blood dripping from her nose, and she's unconscious.

"You cursed her."

It's the only explanation.

Cursing is a form of magic that's most commonly found in Unseelie. The Seelie kingdoms generally abhor it as something that their darker, blighted brethren might conjure, and they keep their fingers well clear of it.

But I spent years in Unseelie.

I know what a curse looks like.

Adaia cursed her to forget me.

I can't breathe. I can't fucking breathe. The daemons inside me howl and scream. And for a second my vision goes black.

Curses are borne of magic, but they're twined of hatred.

It doesn't matter how much power you have when you lay a curse. A common hag can spit a curse so powerful it withers the ground around her for fifty miles, if she's emotionally connected to the curse she speaks.

Curses brew in hate. They smolder with resentment. And they find fertile ground in feelings of betrayal.

The angrier you are when you speak the curse, the stronger it is. The more you hate the person you curse, the more it lingers. The death of the curser can undo a curse in some instances—usually after a few months or years as those feelings dissipate and the curse unknots—*if* the emotions that breathed it into the world weren't too strong.

A curse that is spoken in pure rage and betrayal—one that eats enough of your magic—can linger long beyond the death of the curser.

I curl Vi against my chest, pressing a kiss to her temples.

Curses can always be broken.

It's just a matter of finding the right key to unlock it.

And then Mariana is there, gently stroking a hand through Vi's hair. Her eyes go vacant as she magically probes Vi, and then she gasps.

"What is it?"

Mariana looks troubled. "Who has done this to her? Her mind is laced with enough barbs that they're tearing her to pieces."

"Can you fix it? Can you heal her?"

"Not here. I need my full circle of seven behind me." Mariana bites her lip. "It's bad, my prince. I think I can save her life but I don't know… if there will be any long-lasting damage."

Damage. The enormity of the situation hits me as I surge to my feet with Vi in my arms.

Adaia merely smiles. "Long live true love."

"You fucking—"

Thalia grabs me by the arm. "Vi," she snaps. "We need to get her home. We need to get her back to Ceres. Now. None of this matters."

"Is this what you call good faith?" I demand of the other queens, both of them watching emotionlessly. "She has *cursed* my wife."

Maren glances beneath her lashes at Adaia. "I saw no curse. I only saw her faint when she saw you. It seems her love for you has faded, Thiago."

I stare helplessly at Lucidia.

She leans on her cane, her face ruthless and implacable. "You swore to abide by the treaty," she tells me. "You should have been clearer in your demands of the Queen of Asturia."

I never expected she would turn her own daughter's brain to mush.

I stare down at Vi.

She loved me once.

She can love me again.

She just needs to be reminded of what she felt for me.

Adaia thinks she won this round?

Never.

Vi's my hope, my light in the darkness. She's the fucking destiny I've spent my entire life searching for. I won't let a fucking curse tear us apart.

"Thiago?" Thalia lays a hand on my shoulder, searching my face for a hint of my intentions.

"We're going home." I cradle my wife to my chest. Dark hair drapes over my arm like a banner and though her eyelashes flutter, she doesn't wake. "I'm taking my *wife* home."

"Three months, little prince," Adaia mocks. "And if she survives then you must bring her back to me."

Fury curls hot claws within me.

I could kill her now.

I could rip her heart—her soul—out of her chest with but a single thought.

And I want to.

But suddenly Eris stands between us—Eris who knows my Darkness only too well.

Don't, her eyes say.

Vi is all that matters. I'll make her fall in love with me again, even if it takes every day of the next three months. I will heal her. I will protect her.

After all, if this curse is spawned of hate, then love *must* be enough to break it.

We'll find a way.

I have twelve more years before Vi's final choice will set us free of this horror, and even though my head is on the chopping block, I believe in her.

I have to believe in her.

"Power the portal," I snap at Finn.

"It needs time to recharge," he says in a quiet voice.

The power required to shift an entire party from one location to another is immense. While the Hallow draws from the leyline, scholars have argued that the well of power beneath it is not immeasurable. It needs time to bloat with magic again. Time to suck in energy.

I don't have that time.

I carry Vi within the portal. "Follow me when you have the chance," I tell my friends. Carrying one or two people with me will be a lesser drain on the Hallow. "Mariana?"

She hurries to my side.

I stare at the three queens. All my life I've hidden what I am. I've quashed my power down small inside me, forced it within a cage of my own will. But now it unfurls within my chest as if it can sense my fury and my need.

I need you, I whisper to the Darkness, for the first and only time.

Instantly, the world drains of color. The pinprick pain of claws sinks into my mind. *I'm listening.*

We cannot let them see what we are. We cannot betray ourselves, I warn it. *But I need you to power this fucking thing.*

There's a moment where I look down at the woman in my arms and I'm not myself.

It's like I look through another set of eyes—the eyes of something cold and hard and ancient.

She's dying, it tells me.

She's not dying. I will not let her.

You're not the one who can hold Death at bay, it mocks. *Unleash me and I can save her. There's no need to power the portal.*

No. I stand firm. *I know you feel something for her too. I know you're just as drawn to her light as I am. We cannot allow Adaia to snuff out Vi's light. Work with me, this one time.*

There's a long moment of silence.

You can't fend me off forever, it tells me, and then shadows begin to swirl around my feet. *I will power the Hallow. But I will need blood.*

"Cut my palm," I tell Mariana.

She looks at me as if I'm out of my mind.

"Just do it."

One neat little slice across my palm and then blood wells.

Blood is where the power lies, whispers the creature inside me.

"You'll never get it to work," Adaia mocks. "Perhaps one of my healers can assist you? Maybe there will be enough left of her if you let me help."

I look at her and know that the Darkness is staring back at her. Adaia actually flinches. "Know this, Queen of Asturia…. I have played by your rules. I have abided by your terms. I have given my word and I will not break it. But if anything happens to my wife, then I will come for you. We will not face each other over the heads of our armies. I will come for you in the night. I will come for you in your dreams. I will come for you and I will tear you to bloody pieces and there is nothing you can do to stop me."

A dangerous laugh escapes me as I squat down and slam my bloody handprint against the cold stone beneath my feet.

The Hallow ignites.

Several screams meet my ears as the queens stagger back. I stare at Adaia as Edain wrenches her out of the way of the swirl of magic.

"You will pay for this one day, Adaia," I whisper,

knowing that she can hear me. "I promise once. I promise twice. I promise thrice. I will be the end of you. Nothing will take Vi from my side. I give you this promise of Darkness. Keep it close to your heart. Because at the end of our thirteen years, nothing will stay my hand. You think me weak?"

I smile at her.

Darkly.

And then I unleash all that power into the world, feeling the portal suck us into oblivion. I do what no mere fae should ever be able to do.

I power the Hallow myself.

There's a cold pit in my heart as we arrive in the Hallow chamber in Ceres. The sudden cessation of magic makes me stagger and I go to one knee. There's a ringing in my ears. A blind spot in one eye. The voice inside my head is quiet, but something inside my chest feels broken.

It feels like a crack appeared there, somewhere in the prison I've formed around the Darkness.

Are you there? I whisper.

There's no answer.

It's gone. For the moment.

Vi stirs in my arms as if the transfer woke her.

Our eyes meet, her pupils dark enough to blot out the blue of her eyes.

"I promise you this," I whisper in a voice that's not entirely mine. "We will never let you go. We will never allow anyone to hurt you. You are ours. Forever and always."

"My prince?" There's a tentative hand on my sleeve.

Mariana.

I blink and color drenches the world. "Here. What do you need?"

"Are you all right?" she asks. "You sounded different for a moment."

Forever and always. It's a strange echo in my head.

Enough to make me search again.

Hello?

Silence.

It's gone. Definitely gone. Buried down so deep I can barely feel it. I take a deep breath. "Take me to the healers. We need to break this curse."

I will have Vi back.

No matter what I must do.

And if the curse doesn't break?

Then I will win her heart all over again.

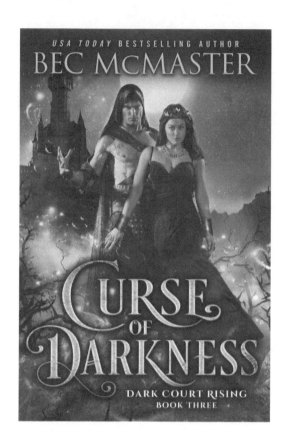

The Darkness is coming…

Iskvien must face her darkest challenge yet, in order to save her world.

Her husband.

Coming September 2021

ABOUT THE AUTHOR

Kidnapped by a dread pirate when she was a child, USA Today Bestselling Author, **BEC MCMASTER**, was raised on myth and legend, and offered her younger siblings to the goblin king many a time. Unfortunately, he did not accept.

Now she writes epic fantasy romance with a dark and sexy twist, which is almost as much fun. She has a secret weakness for villainous heroes, wicked fae princes and dangerous vampires, though in all her daydreams she's the one rescuing them.

Bec lives happily-ever-after with her very own hero and princess-in-training in the wilds of Australia, where she can often be found drinking tea or plotting her next travel adventure.

Escape the ordinary at www.becmcmaster.com

Made in United States
Troutdale, OR
09/20/2024

23004796R00137